Sunshine in the Catacomb

38 Short Stories
by
E.R. Schiller

Original Edition Published in 2015© & Second Printing: 05 June 2020©

ISBN: 978-0578704852

Table of Contents

Author Statement

This collection of 38 short stories initially came from a compilation of 50 I completed between the ages of 17 to 19. I ceased writing fiction after graduating with a BA in English from Temple University, Summa Cum Laude & Phi Beta Kappa member. I do not miss writing. I devote all my free time to drawing now, which can be observed in my other book, *A Record of Madness*. This collection of stories is revised and presented here in faithful form to its initial print years ago. Some stories from the initial collection were edited, shortened, or completely removed for this final edition.

Nobody'd Know Except Me

As Reprinted from *A Record of Madness*©

I stole her wallet. We were sitting in Dr. Shapiro's waiting room and she stood up to get a paper cone cup of water from the cooler and my hand slipped in. Her purse was open. Just like that. Like I'd been doing it all my life. I took it. Fat with credit cards, gift cards, membership cards, insurance cards. Its side was bumpy with change. Something like a meaty fish Jim might've caught last spring. But she was turning around fast, and my purse was too small to fit it so I threw it up under my dress between my thighs. The cranberry leather stuck cold against my skin. It was July then. Inez didn't know me yet.

Angie two houses down suggested Dr. Shapiro to me. She said she used to see him a couple years back. She said there was no harm in admitting when you couldn't take anymore, that the world gave women enough to endure as it was and I'd had too much for anybody. Tuesdays she'd come over. We'd have something strong and fruity to take the edge off. We'd smoke and lean elbows on the orangey shrimp-pink Formica countertop in my kitchen. We'd play scrabble and I'd always win. Angie said Mark saw Jim exit a disreputable lounge in town.

One night I heard Jim outside my bedroom door, listening to see if I was awake. I liked games, I liked catching him, so I sat still and held my breath until his steps receded down the hall. I heard the screen door leading to the front porch clap shut. At my window I watched.

"Am I early?" A man's voice said in the dark. I didn't hear what Jim said back. He got in the car and they sat there. The man turned the engine on but then turned it off. Some little picture inside me glued together the pieces.

After Jim left for work the next morning, I spent an hour brooding at the piano. A 1947 Wurlitzer Spinet. It was the only thing my mother left me before Daddy killed her. He used a crossbow in '62. After it penetrated her body it went through the brown leather recliner she loved so much into the grooved cedar wall behind it. Then I met Jim. He liked the way I played so we didn't sell it off.

My mother had me at forty-seven. I get the image in my mind that she was somebody consigned to a childless fate before I appeared. I was just some globe under her sundress while she chiseled at a crossword puzzle right over my head. At thirteen, Daddy told me he never liked only children. That they never learned to share, that they were missing something fundamental in their nature.

Dr. Shapiro's waiting room was like a big fridge. Air conditioned and crème walls, surgical light and quiet except for a fluorescent tube in the ceiling that would flicker and hum like a nerve. I wouldn't take the medication. I didn't want to be like Jim's sister, Flora, in bed all day. Somebody in me twenty years before might've looked to God for all the answers, but I didn't care anymore. If there was a God, what could I do about it? If there wasn't one, what could I do about it? The radio behind the receptionist's Plexiglas station was squawking about Reagan's speech in June. All peanut butter tan, squared shoulders, red tie and no feasible satisfaction in sight.

I felt hostility towards Inez the first time I saw her. She was plucking up magazines from a spalted sycamore table, old issues of celebrity gossip rags, and tearing out pieces. Strips of glossy paper fell across her lap like hanks of smooth long hair. There was a grace, a clarity to her sweeping wrist. And I hated her for it. For destroying something that wasn't hers. Something I didn't give a damn about until the very moment she disfigured it and made it irreversibly hers.

But a beautiful thing happened. Her fingers fluttered and folded the paper, transforming strips into paper animals. A squat rooster, a sullen cat, all creatures that Benny would have loved. Studying the origami critters, a sadness rose in me. My life tasted gray, but I savored it because I knew it was mine and mine alone to chafe against.

An isolated incident. That's what the police called it. They never caught the person who did it. To my Benny. Five years earlier. Scared the whole town. Benny was a boy who would hoot and howl on the sidewalk, walking into the streets if you weren't holding his hand. It irritated people, when they would say "Hello Benny!" extra-loud like he was deaf, while his eyes rolled around at everything else that wasn't the person talking to him.

The person who took Benny in their car that March morning must've known his fondness for animals, how he loved them because they didn't expect anything of him. It was unbearable. First, they found an eyeball on the playground. Somebody had placed it on the seat of a swing like a wrinkled grape. Then they found a finger, stiff like a baby carrot, tucked behind somebody's windshield wiper. I was certain it was any other child but mine until Parrot Gaskins from across the street rang our doorbell. Her hand was holding one of his white Keds with the laces missing. Her palm was flat open, balancing the shoe in its center like an offering I was supposed to burn.

The laces were what they used, whoever they were, that's what I was later told. I let Jim go down to the pond when we got the call. I stayed behind, folding laundry before the large window in the living room. Trying not to be consumed, I watched Parrot Gaskins' teenage daughter across the street dash to a car at the curb. A boy got out and opened the door for her. I was hungry, transfixed. And I imagined being in the very room of these teenagers. I could see it quite clearly. Them: groping each other under an itchy blue quilt while I sat in a corner chair, smoking in jealousy and sniffing the air and its pockets of cologne, their bodies clutched under careful speculation. Then I pull out my crossbow.

Inez didn't answer my first four knocks. But I never thought it was a mistake coming there. She lived in a row home in the working-class part of town. I saw a flower pot in a tire, dry wiry plants, and a flag's shadow thrashing on the cement walkway. There was a yellow mailbox painted with hummingbirds leaning into the street, hit by a plow in last winter's snow storm. Inez didn't recognize me when she opened the door.

That thrilled me. I could have been anybody. An unidentified woman selling magazine subscriptions. An altruistic schoolmarm registering neighbors to vote. A serial killer. A chronic masturbator. Tall, thin, early forties, good teeth.

"Hi, I'm sorry to disturb you but you left this in Dr. Shapiro's office this morning. You can call me

Bets," and even though I was holding her wallet out to her, just like how Parrot Gaskins had held Benny's shoe out to me, Inez didn't take it. She looked at my face without hearing my words and then we both broke into laughter at the prolonged silence. Who knew it was so easy?

Inez talked quickly. She wanted to tell you everything the way a lonely person might. Being older than her probably helped. Courtesies were exchanged, my address and marital status. The commotion of her words made a strand of hair fall in her eye. Black with flecks of gold. Burning. I noticed a big green plastic bottle of gin next to an empty hamster cage. Gasoline, practically.

She was only 27. She told me she had an art degree but worked in customer service at Tinkle Town Cat Food ® reading and responding to customer letters. She said the previous week several people had written letters pretending to be their pets, Mr. YumYumz or SlutCake, talking about how much they loved Tinkle Town's liver pâté. Her interests ranged from surrealist erotica to obscure documentaries about the South Yemen Civil War.

"Say Bets, do you know where I can buy a cheap vintage wedding dress? I'm looking for one for a photoshoot next weekend."

"Are you going to be wearing it or just taking the pictures?"

"Both."

"Well you look just about my size and I still have mine. I can look for it if you'd like?"

"Can you? That'd be great."

Later that day I went into the basement. It was where Jim had been spending his weekends. I kept my wedding dress down there along with our taxes. But where were the birdhouses he promised me for that summer? There wasn't a single nail in sight. I found a magazine with women in black brocade lace with testicles. Unsmiling, unblinking women gripping conical-shaped contraptions. The issue was dated four months before Benny died. I used to wonder if Jim blamed me for giving him a disabled son or if he felt relief when he died.

After I put the magazine back under a pile of Jim's business-inspiration books (titles like *How You Can Seal the Deal!* or *Make Them Buy!*), I tripped on a roll of Christmas wrapping paper at the foot of the steps. The first fall.

Angie two houses down took me to lunch because the air conditioning in the house was broken. Throughout the night Jim and I had been maintaining a silent war of turning it on and off. At the mall, Angie ate squid ink pasta that made her teeth gray when she opened her mouth to talk. My eyes slid from the tablecloth to the mulberry damask wallpaper and a waitress leaning against it, her black tie askew from the pearl buttons of her blouse. Her ambivalent stare recalled Inez.

"Bets, you need to talk to Jim about this. You don't want him getting that virus on the news. Have you seen the pictures of those people? They look like lepers," Angie's gerbil-brown eyes held me extra-long like she meant it.

"I can't talk to him about it. Not yet," I drank my wine. In my mind an unnamed woman in a white mantle kept appearing, her face averted in her shoulder. Angie stared at me and changed the subject.

"Mark got a call the other night and there was a 400-pound woman that had a heart attack. She hadn't left her house in years. Mark said it was filthy. Just take out containers everywhere. There aren't enough ambulances so what do they do? They bring a firetruck to your front door if you have a heart attack. And the woman was dying and none of the men were trained for that so..." but I didn't hear the rest. Mark was an insurance adjuster at the same firm as Jim. Mark had come back from Vietnam thirteen years before. He'd worked at a summer camp until he was fired the previous summer. He'd make kids stare at the lightbulb in the ceiling of their cabin for hours when they Misbehaved.

Angie proposed seeing the new Cher movie in theaters but I said no. Angie asked how things were going with Dr. Shapiro and I said fine. Angie frowned at her plate. The restaurant wasn't as good as last time. I was starting to understand myself. Perceiving permanency where there was none.

"I've been having these awful nightmares for months since Budd Dwyer shot himself on T.V." I said this in a trance.

"Can you imagine if any kids saw that? What's this world coming to?"

We strolled around the mall an hour before dusk. In a department store we passed a male mannequin, apricot complexion, gray eyes serene. A cold critical glance, wide mouth, the nose a perfect little ski slope. It wore a ribbed black pullover with the sleeves bunched up over the elbows. It wore a stainless-steel Timex on its left wrist. Jim never wore a watch but my father used to.

He had a Bulova with a mother of pearl face. He liked them because they were used to time bombs during the war. Always accurate and unquestionable. It had a rosy brown crocodile leather watchband. When I saw the watchband on that wrist rush toward my face in a fight, a little voice inside me would tell me to clench my teeth, to get angry and quiet about it so I didn't cry in front of him. When he screamed, I wondered who he saw me as. The enemy, the insolent square-jawed German, or the silent wilted Jew?

One of my earrings fell out as Angie and I passed a toy store. As I knelt to the white tile, I looked up Angie's knee length beige wool skirt and felt a pang of shame. Then I looked at her face to see if she'd seen me. But she hadn't. She was staring at the children. I knew she wanted some but couldn't have any. Then a cross-eyed babbling child pattered by and Angie gazed at me with sad sympathetic eyes that made me want to saw her head off with my car keys.

A little boy threw a rock at my car when I parked outside Inez's place the next day. He ran off before I could do anything. I was holding a large cardboard box. Its corners were orange with dust. Images of cinematic splendor invaded my thoughts. Inez perched upon the railing of an elegant estate. Inez stretched on a teal velvet cabriole sofa. Inez crouching, patting a gray fern and staring back at me with a deep satisfaction. Inez wading in a pond, the white hem of the dress lolling in the water. Benny facedown nearby.

"You brought it!" Inez shrieked. I smiled with an almost motherly pride. We sat in her lily pad beanbag chairs and I gave her the box. Her mouth tightened like a scab on my soul when she turned the fabric over in her hands.

"Don't you like it?" I asked.

"It's beautiful...It's just not really my style."

"Oh, that's fine," and my hands slid over hers and took the dress. A shame surged through me, as if my own marriage had been exposed. An urge to flee, a flight from life flowed out of me. I stood up quickly and I couldn't see, the blood in my head made the colors conceal my vision. I was momentarily blinded and my world became something like a rudimentary photograph, tearing into shadows, clouded.

"I've upset you. I didn't mean to upset you," she touched my arm but that didn't stop me from moving my feet. I couldn't see them and I fell on her glass coffee table. I was surprised by how vibrant my own blood was. I could age but my blood would always be young. My palms were stippled with crystal. The second fall.

Inez drove a white Ford Escort with the Madonna painted on the hood, her robes the color of fruit. Banana. Lime. Shielded under an arc of white stars, it rained. Inez had painted the car for her mother who died of malignant cervical polyps eight months before. Inez shouted at traffic and I was touched. All this mayhem for me.

"Should I call your husband or something?" She asked as I sat in the white bed we'd been led to. The sea foam linoleum tiles had an industrial cheese smell. I heard something beeping behind a paste gray curtain. There was a red cart with a beige bin for depositing needles. In the hall was a corkboard that listed stroke warnings. An old woman told an RN nearby that she ran a very fine hotel.

I found myself engrossed, watching them sew my skin without feeling it. Looking at my own arm on the powder blue tissue like a piece of deli meat. A moon-shaped stitching below my elbow, a snipped black wire that reminded me of the occasional chin hair I'd find on myself. Inez left for half an hour while this happened. Blood overwhelmed her.

When she returned something beautiful happened. Her eyes seemed to float just over my face and she kissed my forehead. The pine smell of gin was on those lips. She looked down at me. Inez became a shivering beam of light in the secret mutiny against my morals. A light that reveals a path to a greater joy but with its bright disclosures, forbids the path it alludes to. Her eyeshadow sparkled in the light. Tropical pink frosted on her brow bone, silvery blue on the lids, girlish. It reminded me of myself when I was seventeen.

1962. Inez would've been two at the time. I wore a pair of fake eyelashes that stuck out of my face like whiskers. Daddy hated it. I was on my back on the kitchen floor and he had his knees in my chest, trying to pluck them off my eyes. Mom was clawing at his blonde hair and shouting. He got off me and she went into the living room, sat down in her recliner. Later that night, Jim found me while I was walking in the dark. His car slowed and he let me in. Introduced himself, said he was visiting a senile aunt around those parts. Somebody that might help him pay for college. He had taken a summer job scraping paint off boats at the docks forty-five miles away but ended up spending all the money on the orange mustang he was driving.

I remember. His headlights rode up my legs and I stood in the street, burrs from the sweet gum trees clinging to my socks. Fingers plucking at darkness.

Inez took me back to her place and I slept on an old blue futon beside an empty hamster cage by the front door. Didn't bother to call Jim. He would only come home if he thought I was there. I fell asleep and dreamed he and I were alone together in his old car on the dark curving road a mile from my parents' house. While driving, our headlights caught the face of a disheveled girl walking on the side. We kept going. Then we saw another. And another. Until we saw dozens of small dirty faceless girls dragging themselves forward. At the end of the road was a hunched beast the size of a house eating them by the handful. In the dark I couldn't see what it looked like but only knew how big it was.

Woke up in the night. Inez sat in the kitchen smoking. Several newspaper origami animals stood in a circle around her mineral green glass ashtray. The wedding dress was laid across a walnut slat back stool. Its fitted lace bodice brushed the red checkered floor tiles. Wandering around, I studied a gray skin of grease congealing to a frying pan on the stove. A chipped enamel mug lay on its side in the cast iron sink. And she turned and looked at me. And she rose with an uncertain dignity. And she came to me.

And a vague dread came over me, a renewed fear that this very moment was the duplicate image of something maimed from another life. Guilt entered me. All my private defeats and minor suicides collected around my feet like shed thorns and I couldn't take a single step in any direction without hurting someone. That the delta of veins inside her arm, the russet of sunburn on her cheeks, was just a symptom of something else. Something secret. Something terrifying. Like a hand inside a glove. You know it's there but you know it's only a form.

And I left. Got in my station wagon and drove past the house. 898 Aconite Drive. No lights on. Jim's car absent. White house, blue garage doors, three pink azalea bushes in the front, a wicker peacock chair on the porch and a wasp's nest forming at the chimney. Behind the house, under the pignut hickory that lost half its branches in last year's snow storm, was a swing set partially disassembled.

Benny was once sitting on it and I was once watching him through the back window while reading on the tufted gray leather chesterfield. I was reading a Victorian novel, some story about a tormented heroine that kills herself. In the back, I saw Benny stand up from the slide, his hands slapping against the thighs of his red corduroy overalls. He appeared to be talking to himself. My eyes returned to my book. I was brooding. I had thought about trying to go to college. But it felt like the walls were closing in on me.

I'd tried having a job around then as a saleswoman for Alcoa, selling knife kitchenette sets and cooking tools. Door to door and phone calls. I'd get a fifteen percent commission for every sale. Jim wanted to encourage me by being my first customer. He bought the most expensive item in my kit: a pearl handled seven-inch meat cleaver and its plum leather sheath for $66.37. I'd get dressed for work in my punch colored Ponte blazer and Jim would wave me towards the door with a smile like a kid going to their first day of school. But the babysitter quit on us. Then the next. One night there was something on the news about kids with disabilities being a result of inadequate maternal bonding and Jim told me maybe I should go back to work when Benny got into school.

The headlights of my car made a white catwalk on the wet asphalt in the dark. Devo's "Too Much Paranoias" was on the radio. Almost a decade since I had first heard it with Jim, I recalled the day we listened to it when I was seven months pregnant. He hid the record in brown wax paper behind his back while walking toward me. At that time, it was eleven years after our courthouse wedding and I was afraid I would be like my mother and have a child at fifty. I had been thinking about going to college but when it came to applying, a piece of me would go stale and silent. I got pregnant. It got put off. That day as Jim brought the record to me, I was staring at myself in the mirror. I looked like an alien. I suddenly became aware of how bizarre my own body was. That I was a bloated amphibian, hosting this creature inside me. And some screaming purple goblin would be given to me and I would be told to love it.

But that was long gone. In my car, Alice Cooper took over the radio and those gloomy kids in town with their safety-pinned earlobes and ripped fishnets on their wrists flashed through my mind. Drinking in each other's lips behind a pharmacy and flicking the ash off their laps. In the night, the deep night as I was alone with the radio, with the dashboard knobs like blue choking candies under my fingers, I decided to find Jim. My Jim. At the Nieve Roja. Thirty-five miles rushed into me.

It was obvious I was new. I was wide-eyed. There were ten people sitting and standing when I arrived. The place hadn't been renovated for a decade. The walls were covered with avocado green polyester carpets, like a giant uncontrollable sea anemone. We were inside it. We were chosen by its vicious hunger. There was a man in pecan plaid trousers and an ivory sweater vest, his hair parted to the far left to conceal a receding hairline. As he spoke his front teeth would dart out from the shelf of his blonde moustache. His hand clenched and unclenched the handle of a brown leather briefcase. Jim was speaking to him and standing next to a fringed white macramé lamp, eyes shifting toward the entrance. He hid his shock well and approached me. Perhaps that was a talent that made me marry Jim, an ability to seemingly disappear without going anywhere.

"My name's Indigo, come sit," Jim said. Indigo wore a black demi-plunge corset, the lavender bows of her brassiere were protruding from a cerulean tank top and a rhinestone burette had fallen to her earlobe after a shot of whiskey, like a comet in her polyurethane locks. Oh Indigo. I fell for her artillery of hollow pearls and amethyst rings. I was impaled on her tube of mascara and I was terrorized by longing. I smelled the vanilla tang of my own perfume on her shoulders that she had given me last Christmas.

We sat in a fungus-yellow suede tub chair that groaned beneath us when we swiveled in it. At our knees was a Danish teak square coffee table with a copper blue ashtray. Hiding the sore stitches on my right arm with my opposite hand, I stared at the top of Indigo's corset, a black scalloped lace trim on top that blended into her chest hair. I felt plain and faded next to Indigo, clinging to my cheap pigskin purse. All these years I had never tried to wear nice lingerie in our marriage. I sat staring at a tear in her pantyhose and felt possessive over my own ugly isolated womanhood.

Our eyes held each other in a dark disembodied embrace that became the still point of the ever-turning world. I felt a gradual subtraction of identity as if all was known and there were no distinctions. The prism of language subsided as I suffered the patient injuries of an angel. Indigo was my silent sea bride. After studying her, my interest slackened. Because like all peripheral objects, they become familiar. The road becomes turned too many times, the corner of the page creased and stained.

"Don't come home," I told Indigo, avoiding her eyes and staring at the acne scars on her cheeks that looked like somebody had poked the skin over with a needle.

"Bets, I know this is tough. But I'm not hiding anymore. I just couldn't tell you. Sometimes I think you're the most intense person I've ever met."

"Then you don't know a lot of people."

Scenes of total irrelevance flashed through my brain, of myself and the way I feverishly polished furniture while Benny cried on the rug behind me. I: myself: placing a lidded pot of my mother's recipe stew on a lace doily at the table, a thousand wet shivering eyes clinging to its surface. Beef cubed by a cleaver. A cracking noise that made me wince.

My cuffs tightened at my wrists. My anxiety was a sound emitted at ultrasonic range. My eyebrows raised in surprise. The colors were bubbling up. The colors were coming for me. Swamp black and lye white. Cantaloupe pink and strangled purple. And I left Indigo. I left the person I found when I left my parents.

1962. I was about to graduate high school. I was in our church's rec center ballroom, standing on the grey veined marble in a satin toothpaste green dress. Two men in suits with red carnations in their lapels each held a sword over their heads making an arc. We were instructed to walk under them. Our fathers recited a covenant to protect us and we kneeled before a wooden cross draped in white. A vow of purity before marriage. It was like a prom only our fathers took us. Elena Marber. Denise Deagon. Zipporah Phillips. All in white, twirling around the cross, their crinoline petticoats fluttering. White spots refracted in the black brass chandeliers overhead, the gold maple leaf wallpaper ablaze.

A purity ball, a ceremony to celebrate our chastity. I had overheard a couple girls in my high school call me a Christ freak, that I was brainwashed by old parents. Already a poor student, their rejection was a permanent pain like glass embedded in skin. Fuming with so much determination, I went out and bought some makeup and fake eyelashes at the five and dime after school. I'd just painted my face for the first time and I didn't want to go home. I stumbled on a couple kids in the woods near my house, a bit younger than me, sitting around a bonfire burning their schoolwork. Two boys, one girl. I watched a boy crush a beer can into a hockey puck and a girl nibble her cuticles. Then they started kissing and the second boy turned to me. When I came home my cheeks were purpled with lipstick. My stockings rolled down my calves and smelled like wood smoke.

A nasal record of the Ink Spots was playing in the living room that night. My mother saw me but said nothing. She burned the meatloaf because she forgot about it while crowing at her sister on the telephone. My father wouldn't eat pork because it reminded him of the bodies in the war. He was in a foul mood because a woman at the power plant stepped on his glasses when they slid off his nose while he was tying his shoe. He said that women knew what they were doing, that they could be just as cruel as men. I sat at the kitchen table that night admiring my reflection in a brass teapot on the stove.

My face was pink with delight and my father noticed it in a vicious wordless stare. In my gunmetal blue eyeshadow, he saw the woman in the factory. He saw his own mother that died when he was nine. Saw the Great Whore of Babylon. The spittle on his trembling lip terrified me when he yelled. And he got on me. And my mother tried to stop him. She said she liked my makeup. He asked her if she knew about my smeared lipstick. She screamed at him, told him he was insane, that he didn't know when to shut up, when to stop. He looked at my mom like she'd betrayed him. He went out to the garage where he kept his wood saws and paint cans. A yellow island of light settled on the grass where he had opened the front door, the crossbow hanging between his knees.

I ran from the house. A boy in an orange mustang pulled over and asked me what was wrong. He was kind to me. He let me stay with him and his family. I'd always feel a debt to him. I could never have been with anyone else.

Daddy, don't do this for your God.

Angie was sitting on my porch when I came home. I saw a winking red eye in the dark and knew she was smoking. She gripped the wedding dress against her chest while she spoke.

"I've been waiting here for a little bit. I hope you don't mind. I just needed to talk. Some girl dropped this off by the way. She seemed nice, pretty too," Angie smirked at the dress in her hand, "It's a little dowdy, don't you think?", and flicked the lit head of her cigarette into the azalea bush. I made gin and lemonades as Angie sat on the harvest gold linen sofa, sleepily admiring the bookshelves with a hand in her auburn hair. She wore floral printed silk pajamas under a blue cardigan. A pair of red sponge flip-flops looked up at her from the yellowing rug, matted in the center and concealing crumbs from crackers.

"I was putting away Mark's shirts today and I found this in his drawer," she pulled out a plastic baggie and at first, I thought they looked like little yellow chords all tangled up. Then I saw the puckering brown heads of mushrooms.

"Angie, you have to put that back before he finds out."

"Who says? You're no fun. Bets, look at this. Do you want to try it with me? I'm afraid to do it alone," her head was cocked to the side and she gazed up at me with a childish magnetism. I closed my eyes and felt her thin soft fingers part my lips. Bitter. Gummy in some places, paper dry in others.

The hum of the fridge was the grind of the moving earth and I cried for every little thing in this world I wanted to love but didn't know how to. The burning medallions of my eyes craved light. Bright flooding light. Clean soundless light. I lay down on the sofa. It felt five feet above the carpet.

"Angie, who are you talking to?" She was standing in the corner, her hands were agitated, curling into fists, flattening into karate chops, emphasizing some whispered interaction. "They put the pieces back in me wrong," she kept saying. A botched abortion. No more kids. I held her close and felt her frenzied pulse against my blouse. Her head drooped to my shoulder.

We smiled as I walked her home that night. She clung to my arm with a breathless urgency. Somebody ran over a raccoon earlier and we stood in the middle of the street staring at its leveled black carcass. Tufts of brown fur seemed to grow out of the asphalt and a gray claw stuck through the purple clay of its dried blood. On her doorstep she stroked my arm and discovered the scaly divots of stitches under my elbow, she looked but didn't ask. We embraced.

An eerie silence filled my house. A place I had learned and understood better than my own spouse, with walls and halls and doors and windows that witnessed our sick fashions of love and laughter in speechless agreement. The wedding dress was rumpled on the striped divan in the hall, a black line of dirt on its hem. Nobody wants you now.

And then I was naked. My nipples hardened like little pink knots in the air conditioning. My hands hovered over the black lacquered frame of the mirror in the dining room. My eyes studied the magenta band of my cesarean scar dipping downward, above my pubic hair. The speckled green wall behind me leered at my disappearing back dimples. I had found my primitive self. My name wasn't Bets. I wasn't forty-two. I was not real.

Up the steps and down the hall was a special place nobody could enter but me. The door had a hole in it from when I'd thrown my shoe at Jim while fighting. Later, Jim filled it with gray putty that didn't even match the white paint on the door. Inside everything was untouched. His yellow dinosaur pillowcase still had the indent from his small head. I'd even left the dirty laundry on the floor. His green Velcro sandals from the beach were parted at the bottom of the closet, straps undone as if he'd just been standing in them.

The stranger took Benny to the pond he loved so much before he died. They must've known my boy. It was the good part of the pond, where the geese sat and hissed at you for bread, not the bad part where the teenagers left their condoms in the mud like milky jellyfish. Perhaps the stranger was fast about it. Didn't push his pudgy cheek into the pebbled mud at the water's edge. Didn't take his fingers off until he stopped breathing.

A school aid? Counselor? Recess chaperone? Neighbor? Drifter? Demi-God?

I thought he was talking to someone when he was on the swing set and I was hiding inside, moping and jobless. I did get frustrated. Once a thunderclap scared him and he knocked over a ceramic vase. He'd crawl into my bed at sunrise with wet pajamas. It angered me sometimes. To spill all my love into a child that couldn't reciprocate, couldn't speak or listen. I didn't smoke or drink while I was pregnant, I wanted to find patterns that could justify why my child was different. But there was nothing.

Just once, I visited my father in prison. We sat at a green poplar card table decorated by the black half-moons of cigarette burns. The pock-marked cement walls chilled me. My mind felt my fingertips sting at the thought of touching them. His hair had gotten thin, from blonde to ash. I despised him. I loved him.

"How are things?"

"Fine. I'm married with a son now."

"What's he like?"

"Complicated. We've been seeing a lot of doctors lately."

"What's wrong with him?"

"We don't really know."

"Maybe God is punishing you."

Benny's room felt warm, the air wasn't moving in it. A sealed off tomb, preserved out of guilt by me. The corner of an etch-a-sketch peeked from underneath the bed, its red frame collecting dust. A Stretch Armstrong doll lay on its back on the brown nylon carpet, its arms open and legs spread, sporting a black speedo, like he was enjoying a patch of sun on the French Riviera and not the dirty floor of a dead boy's bedroom. I was afraid Benny would've been disregarded and pitied by children and adults. That he would've bagged groceries and pushed carts for pennies his entire life thinking he didn't matter to society. They never found his killer.

Slumped on his bed, in my body I saw my mother's body, poached in her living room armchair. All those morbid nights from the past, where she would lock the door upstairs with the bathtub running for hours but come out dry and quiet. And I heard those little noises she made in the house, the clicking of bone needles and sighs.

I left Benny's room. Downstairs, in the kitchen, I opened and closed the drawers. Every item was new before me, unfamiliar apparatuses used to cut apart skins and muscles and meats that I consumed. And then something beautiful happened. It appeared before me, unassuming and untouched. A plum leather pouch my fingers lingered over, lingered over the way I could've done to Inez.

Images surfaced in my mind of Budd Dwyer shooting himself on T.V, of suicide revenge fantasies, of jumping off a building and my head on the pavement like a smashed cupcake, of thoughts of myself not knowing I existed unless I inflicted some degree of pain, of Inez in wildfires and plane crashes. Land burning for miles. Mounds of flesh raining from the sky and eaten by wolves. My mother and Benny and some evil symmetry running through my life like a seam of acid.

I pressed my bare knees against the white melamine kitchen cabinets. My left-hand lay limp on the orangey shrimp-pink Formica countertop. My right hand drifted toward the Brazilian rosewood cutting board.

Maybe I did resent my child. Nobody'd know except me. There was a relief in holding the cleaver. It could split up the false patterns. It was turning day outside. A train rumbled by in the distance. A little black bird flew from a tree and was never seen again.

Man of Exits

1.

His specialty was sex crimes. He did not have any friends in this new city he had moved to. A tall, thin, quiet man, Severin had a chin like a slab of granite, a bald spot on the back of his head whose sweat would catch the light like one pale egg in a flaxen nest. He picked his ear with his eyeglasses as his lingering dispassionate gaze settled over the photographs on his desk he'd been given that morning, of ligature marks on the throat of a man named Clark Kistemakker. The images intrigued him. He was talented at his work. A decade previous he had seen an assortment of ugliness while overseas that had hardened him to such sights. Once he saw a man with his leg blown off and the bone jagged like a snapped off toothpick. In the photograph on his desk, Clark Kistemakker's face was bloated like a white mushroom. His mistress, a Soledad Woolridge, sat across from Severin.

2.

She pulled the gray coat he'd given her in the patrol car over her bruised shoulder. He poured more coffee to keep her talking. That was his job back then. Get them cozy. Get them talking. But don't give them any promises.

"When did you first meet Mr. Kistemakker?" he asked.

"When I was twenty at the Nyxia. I had bumped into an old high school friend of mine, Patty Mass, in the parking lot of the grocery store near my apartment. She and I hit off again and we went out to dinner, she told me about it, that I would like it if I gave it a try."

"I see" He nodded while scribbling on a clipboard but he was actually writing nothing. Sometimes when his pen jerked in rapid yet composed motions on paper it made them quiet, let it set in for them, that they're here and not leaving anytime soon. Soledad asked if he had a cigarette. He told her he quit ten years ago. A small lie to keep her still.

3.

Soledad Woolridge, twenty-five, morgue receptionist. Job summary consisted of admitting and releasing cadavers from the county morgue. Assisting pathologists in autopsies, transferring bodies to storage units, routine paper work, confirming details of identity, entry level salary of 30k.

4.

Severin was amused by the random humanness of her recollection. Of bumping into an old friend in a simple place, her hands clinging to the toothpaste green plastic handle of her shopping cart, setting up a dinner date and learning of a new place, a new world that would scoop her up, out of an isolated existence. Nyxia: the web page described it as an improvisational interactive theater. Eighteen to enter and admission $20. Black screen with pink curling font. 9 pm to 2 am. He imagined it quite clearly: Soledad stopping at a bar nearby to fortify herself with gin, an oak trim bar with a thick epoxy resin lacquer coat, the crack of billiards and the mellow beam of a pendant light hovering over a retro Scandinavian pine stool accompanied by the insinuating stare of a loser at the other end of the room.

5.

A Victorian house with large red church-like doors, Soledad arrived early to acclimate herself to the environment, identify bathrooms and fire exits. She was alarmed by a sensation similar to being in a new country. The first room she entered was called a Little's room. Within was a blanket fort (fleece quilts with a rancid cheesy stench), coloring books, snapped crayons, Disney music, Barbies missing heads and clothes, and a fenced in playpen with chew toys. A fat boy with thick curling lashes and fox ears huddled in a crate. The second room was a wrestling room. Styrofoam mats gray and creased like the sort seen in grade schools. No stilettos permitted while fighting (to avoid punctures). Cold metal foldable chairs the color of chocolate milk surrounded the perimeter. Florescent bulbs and shoulders red from impact resembling sunburns.

6.

She let her imagination meander as she spoke. Words aloud became music and she blushed at Severin with an obscene gratitude for letting her relive her past. She entertained a dream, some erotic obsession that culminated in the ruin of its two united figures. Telling her tale elevated her to a seat of authority. She was the empress. She that presided over corpses. The ash-eater in the dark.

7.

The final room was a medium length ballroom, oak floors, a series of saltire crosses and a DJ in the corner. Thirty people stood around in leather gear chatting and observing one woman fifteen feet away with short blonde hair, a studded vest, meaty hands, and a long heavy elephant whip. When she released it onto the man's body it made the same sort of motion as a frog's tongue catching a fly. Soledad watched with an unrestrained fascination. There was a woman whose body was coiled in rope, suspended mid-air like an archangel from a steel frame platform. There was a gentleman conducting electric play on the opposite side of the room. He had a broad calm face, white hair, a Hawaiian shirt with a variety of clownfish clinging to his pectorals. He would circle a neon hand held wand over one's muscles. It hummed like a bug zapper.

8.

Severin wanted to believe Soledad was just some young woman swept up by the talkative talents of an older man, drawn into his little imaginary web of marble terraces and stainless cutlery. Maybe being with an older man made her think she could prolong her own youth. But she was with the body when they found her. Keep pouring coffee.

9.

"How did his wife feel about your affair?" Severin asked her.

"They reached an agreement after their son died. She let him go with other women so he wouldn't leave her. He still did though. Can I take my shoes off? My feet hurt."

Severin's eyes registered the cuneiform of a zipper imprint crawling up the inside of her calf from her knee-high patent leather boots. Her mouth was waxy with cheap garnet lipstick and her hand, laced in henna, fumbled with her sunglasses like a nervous bird. She had argyle socks tattooed to her ankles. He stared at her green and black tessellated flesh, wondering if the ink extended to her toes. Maybe Clark took Soledad to quicken the fading image of another. She chewed her thumb, which was as red as a bead of molten glass.

10.

"Maybe one of the men around here smokes. You think you could ask one of them for me?"

"In a minute, Soledad." She didn't like that but he did.

11.

Severin identified a shared trait in Soledad that made him despise her. They were both outsiders that had pursued professions to satiate their own morbid predilections. In Fallujah he saw a friend shot in the chest. When it happened, his face didn't display terror or sadness, but confusion. The photograph of Clark Kistemakker didn't have that. There was something vacant and serene there. Perhaps, he thought, Soledad understood. Perhaps for her the strangest part about the Nyxia wasn't what happened there but rejoining the world afterward. Returning to copiers and sawdust coffee, pretending she was fine. She had been nowhere that weekend. Saw nothing and no one. She was simply Soledad, picking a yellow scab off a mosquito bite behind her desk and rolling it between her fingers like a splinter. Soledad, walking the halls and maintaining social equilibriums, yet all the while the glitches inside were clicking and sliding, colliding and dividing. Like a cancer.

12.

On his license Clark Kistemakker had neutral slate blue eyes. Over the years his eyebrows had kept their color while his hair faded, despite its invincible thickness. The walls of his home were decorated with his framed degrees in psychology and conventional portraits. Shoulders gingered by sun freckles on the beach, asleep in a green lounge chair with a blue cap over his face. Another, of his wedding, he smiled with his mouth shut. Another, of the christening of his first and only child who died a year later. The baby's eyes were closed, some sly premonition of what would be and his lips hovered over its head, smoothed out by some devout tranquility, waiting to pluck a kiss. None of these photos were as beautiful as the one the homicide unit had taken of him that morning.

13.

"Shouldn't I have a lawyer with me? In the movies they say you should."

"This isn't the movies, Soledad."

14.

Somebody must've had her secret. Some dead person she talked to at work. Some gnarled inert body that knew what she meant. Maybe the only way she could tell anybody about herself was if she cut them up afterwards and took it out of them. Maybe they knew. About sacrificial violence. About sex and death. About the fleeting things.

15.

During the summer Severin had been enduring a particular period of self-erasure, drinking. Eating out of a microwave for ten days. Ellio's pizzas, a dough rectangle with ice flakes clinging to its tomato edges.

16.

Drinking had forced him to transfer to this new city. A change of scenery didn't change the situation. When he first arrived he was so sure, so resolute. In the morning he'd promise tonight would be the dry night. But he didn't want to go to the AA meetings with all the Christ freaks urging the world to urge with them for an urgent change in the world. He drank in his car because the movie theater was situated in a strip mall with a liquor store and a Chuck- E- Cheese. The place exuded a serious level of austerity in his soul. The image of those mechanical animals on the sound stage appeared before him, their plastic banjos and denim overall hips jerking from side to side. Maybe what disturbed him most were the parents he imagined and their glaring existential dilemmas, shrugging over iced lemonade as the fat kid got stuck in the slide.

17.

In the theater Severin watched a blockbuster rom-com. Some big-name production that three people died to while watching. He found himself laughing at every punch line while some grotesque demon in his brain wondered every waking minute which scene those beautiful innocent people had been laughing at, too, when they had been shot dead by that maniac.

18.

Soledad coughed into her elbow, followed by a pleasant shutter. A cold beauty, a goddess in exile, she frowned at him, and something hopeless appeared. He saw it in her. That same feeling he had when he was five, walking down the sidewalk and a man knocked him down running for the bus. You're on the ground, shocked and scraped, looking up and nobody's there. No mom. No God.

19.

Perhaps Clark Kistemakker had predicted an anonymous death for himself. Cardiac arrest at the bank. Just another fatality in an interstate pileup. Being swept away in a flash flood. Muscles sheared down by a hail of bullets in a movie theater. Some slow pneumonia at ninety. Perhaps he was a man of exits.

20.

His bedroom was aesthetically modern. The walls were tiete rosewood paneling. Fine fabrics of canton crepe silk bedding and course indigo tussah curtains could be discerned. Next to the bed was a crystal table clock on a weathered oak nightstand. Clark Kistemakker was on his back in bed. When they removed the braided jute rope from his throat there was an aubergine necklace in his flesh. Bruises became an outline of a second personality. His milky blue eyes stared forward at a painting on the wall, an image of the ocean serrated by wind. His cheeks were still silver with the moisture of Soledad's glossy swamp flower.

"He liked it that way. We never did it any other way."

21.

Severin rode the train to work. Small overhead screens advertised the oncology department of the local hospital. All tickets and passes out. $7.50, please. Ladies and gentlemen, please be alert to threatening people or suspicious objects. He looked out the window, pretending to be engrossed in the derelict buildings outside to avoid paying. Burnt tangerine sunset with one glorious sun glaring like the end of a cigarette. He turned to the people around him. He was an unabashed starer, like a child. His mind gave them each elaborate histories, metaphysical aspirations, traumatic childhoods, estranged spouses.

22.

Soledad arose in his mind. He imagined her as gangly and bullied growing up. Her chart said she was from the rural part of the state. But she must have always had secrets. She attended a small private women's college nearby with a degree in biology.

23.

On the train, Severin observed one particular old Chinese woman with a red scarf around her wrist, yet he detected an invasive energy on his left side. He glanced over and saw a young woman in sunglasses staring at him. Another shameless voyeur. A fellow interloper. She studied him, strung together the freckles on his forehead like constellations. He smiled at her in a gentle indistinguishable way. A small invitation to keep staring. A coin for the beggar.

24.

His stop came and he stood. One hand gripped the pole by the sliding door. He craned his neck to get a better view of the woman in sunglasses. He had not seen the walking stick under her feet. Yet the woman smiled, like she could feel him thinking about her.

25.

Once as a teenager, Severin went hunting with his father. He killed a doe, skinned and ate it. His father kept its head as a trophy. What nobody knew was that in the blind internal silence of his solitude, Severin confessed himself to this mounted deer head. If he was alone, the strings of the house aligning in its daily labors, he would crouch in a superficial pose of reflection and speak aloud to the animal he had slaughtered. His victim, petrified in formaldehyde, its fur flat and stiff against it scalp, listened with the mute devotion of the dead.

26.

Soledad gazed at Severin. Her bottom lip trembled with the same paralyzed intrigue as the deer. Eyes alive and bearing the weight of anticipation. Every scuffed shoe, every yard of rope, every psychiatric construction and clinical persuasion in Clark Kistemakker's career were merely accessories to his demise. Soledad Woolridge, the tattooed morgue receptionist with her sordid tales of exploitation, her inane sensualism, was a bystander. Severin wanted to despise them both. Especially since her white snakeskin miniskirt reminded him of his Aunt Clarissa.

27.

Severin had one picture of his Aunt Clarissa, on a porch with Uncle Jerry. He was a big man with a feathery patch of red hair whose dwindling existence was compensated by a damp wolfish amount of black arm hair. In the snapshot he's shirtless. Aunt Clarissa is crouched next to him. Her lettuce green satin panties are visible between her knees. Her head is cocked to the side, as if she's listening for the police sirens that would come for Jerry ten months later.

28.

Aunt Clarissa had a mini disco ball from the local party store rotating on her bed when Severin walked in one day at the age of twelve. She called it practicing. She invented a game called office. He was the worker and she was the boss. The first time she kissed him he recoiled. A magazine tear-out of Yvonne de Carlo above the television loomed over their huddled figures.

"That picture makes me nervous," he told her.

"We can fix that." The odor of her breath lingered. She spoke with the deliberate assurance of a sociopathic vixen that had seen the world and tried to recreate it in her bedroom. She jumped from the bed and grabbed a pair of scissors. Several long black hairs clung to the loops where she had trimmed her dead ends the night before. She tugged down the picture, cut out the eyes and put it back on the wall.

29.

The wallpaper underneath was white so Yvonne's eyes became two empty almond-shaped outlines.

"You made it worse."

"It's not there if you don't look at it."

30.

Ladies and gentlemen, please be alert to threatening people or suspicious objects.

31.

"You want to hear something that doesn't matter?" Soledad asked.

He said nothing. She went on.

"I'm sick of your questions. You know what your questions are like? I'll tell you what they're like. Have you ever tried pointing in front of a dog? It's kind of a comical experience. You're pointing and shouting but the dog just keeps staring at your hand. I'm telling you what happened and you just want to tear it up. You're just a dumb dog. Look for yourself."

32.

He pulled out a cigarette and lit it. She remained calm while she spoke.

"Can I have one?"

"No."

Sunshine in the Catacomb

Sitting in the bathtub with my clothes on and the faucet clogged with flesh. Watching the wings of a fly twitch down the cracked tiles, curtains pulled back like splattered ghosts and an alarm going off for two hours. I think about the diving board at the swim club as a kid and that time I hit the water on my back when someone threw a tennis ball at me while I was doing a flip. That smack against my spine as I drifted to the bottom like a widow of Atlantis, a lifeguard cackling. That's what my desperation feels like, after the impact of a fender and you've flown ten feet up, you're in purgatory unaware.

My pencil skirt is clinging to my thighs like an extra layer of black skin and my peach leather heels are filled with purple water. Probably shouldn't still be here, but that's usually how it goes for me. The dull white ceiling is the inside of a skull dripping on my forehead from the steam. There are clumps of ash by the toilet and the handcuffs are draped over the trash can. The checkered floor is strewn with your lime green T shirt, denims with light up sneakers. The housekeeper will be here soon. A painting of the sea shore above the laundry basket is cracked, the frame opened and a little ginger girl kissing a seashell smiling at the wall. A straight razor dangles from the silk bathrobe on the doorknob.

They offered me assistant director of the education department but I turned it down because then I couldn't watch you finger-paint. Mr. Demarvel asked me to sit with him in the lunchroom and even bought me a Snapple. You liked him so much when he threw you over his shoulder and strode down the hall after the spelling bee. He's a good role model, flossed gums and a master's certificate, former line-backer with a scar on his nose from when I crossed my legs.

During an internship in the past, my boss told me I was unique for an employee before I bit his tongue at the Christmas party. Father died of emphysema in February and he wanted a grandchild before he died by shih tzus don't count. Aunt

Catherine moved downstairs to slip him a thimble of bleach in crangrape. We're getting our inheritance to pay the nurses and the lawyers advised us to stay in the area. Aunt Catherine said she saw your soul flutter to the window as she sat by your side, ganja is awesome. The ivory keys on the Steinway in the living room are streaked with emerald scratches from my nail polish and the sofa still has a tear from the Siamese feline I locked out on the porch.

I'm unfolding on the marble, my toes tapping the knobs. I shaved my crotch for Mr. Demarvel and it feels like a cactus and looks like a pink mole, dig me. I remember when we hatched chicks last month and an egg exploded in the incubator and I had to teach you in the music room for a week. Your stubby fingers caressed your sunburned ears from Bermuda on holiday break. I would have kissed that twisted rose-toned flesh on the side of your scalp many a time. When we sat in a circle on the rainbow rug and recited our favorite animals, you said a kangaroo just like me.

Halloween parade I found you sobbing under the basketball net with your cowboy hat over your face. What's wrong? I asked, but the bruises on your arm said it to me already, this was just a chance to get closer to you. Sensitive and loving, you were weaker than the others. Scaly lips from autumn cold curled into your face when I hopped on foot to make you laugh. In high school you would have been one of those kids who cut class to smoke behind the auditorium, vodka Evian in your locker, just like me and our kangaroos.

Combination to my heart was your plutonium green eyes groveling in my Toyota.

Didn't even clean up the mess when I left, I'm okay with prison. Drinking from a box of wine, I feel particularly pitiful though I shouldn't because I've gotten what I wanted out of life. Sioux cigarillos are soaked with your tears and the tokens of your eyes are sealed beneath the foyer. Let the police find what they want. Let the district be severed from funds. Let Mr. Demarvel recoil in horror under his desk. Aunt Catherine you're crazy enough to say you still love me and there are better lies you can tell.

Peyote priests eat flesh to preserve the souls of their loved ones and I did the same, but now your ample skin will be crammed in my bowels temporarily. Sociopath, seductive siren with smiley stickers, is this what I lived to become? Don't blame the principal and don't blame the staff, for who detects the eagle before it swoops down on the nest? Sure, there were good times, but luck is chance and trouble is guaranteed.

Newspaper frenzy will ensue and they'll make me a mockery of monster in the media. My neighbors will say, "She was always so kind, she helped me paint the shutters" or "She was so thoughtful, I could tell her about my retarded canary" or "Who would suspect such a sweet little schoolhouse maiden?" I could walk down the street and flirt with the balding business men at the parking meters, who would have no idea who the fuck they were smiling at. I could unwind in palates class and babysit the instructor's nephew on

Thursdays, entrusting an executioner with glee. Their oblivion was amusing and I will be savagely beaten with my laughs in the asylum.

Carnival of spectral slaves in the United States, behold the freak on your soil, spit at the television screen. Whisper over your shoulders in the bleachers of a baseball game, I stood there with you once too, talking of scandal and serendipity with your mothers and uncles like the community bedsore. Drugstore lines at the register, coffee house laptop pestilence, ATM eleven pm, I was there too just like you. I am your niece and your daughter. I am your neighbor and asswipe who swerved at the intersection. I am your casual acquaintance in the supermarket who discussed taxes over lettuce and carrots. I am your friend and colleague. I am everywhere.

After I changed my clothes and left, I drove to the local park and sat on a bench near the trail, smoking unfiltered cigarettes and nodding at joggers. I kicked up some gravel and talked to God for a couple minutes before I concluded how untraceable my atheist accent had become. Dancing through the vegetation, I urinated by a tree stump, and again nodded to a jogger. A blonde with a ponytail and sports bra, pushed a stroller down the path and I was overwhelmed.

I killed him because I was touched as a child too, only they didn't have the decency to kill me afterwards. When they sit me down at the other side of the table and ask me about it, I shall offer no information but confirm my charges. It's none of their business how that poor tadpole got into my clutches, that's just morbid curiosity and the parents don't need to hear it from me. Surprised by my empathy?

Hanging in the skyline is your face and it's speaking to me. You're screaming all the curse words you know and I am pleased with your progress. I can't stand up from the ground, can't get up out of myself. I'll be expecting you in my dreams and maybe after twenty years I'll feel guilt, but I was too calculating for remorse. My cellmate can throw genesis at me as they drag me across the cement floor by my hair, I'm okay with that. I'm okay with cutting my patties with a spoon for the rest of my life and I'm okay with orange jump suits and evening protocols.

Lights out. Breaking news. I'll disappear in a media whirlpool when another catastrophe replaces me. They'll glorify me briefly with their complete attention, savagely excavating my past and interviewing my relatives on television. Then I'll smile in my cot, pretending it never ended. Believe in the dream, it's plagued everyone. Believe in me, I will return in the face of someone else.

The Most Boring Woman in the World

I've made a habit of watching the most boring woman in the world. Invisibility is her priority. On the train I note the detail of her wardrobe. How intense her inclination to the banal translates in the plainest fabrics. The dullest shades. Her exterior exists out of an anxiety to preserve her facelessness.

Glasses round, thick, rimless. Shoes baby powder white, canvas browning around the edges. High cotton socks. The first time she sat in front of me, she pointed her toes sharply to the floor and pulled out a large green library book. Detecting a tension, I averted my face. Her dark brown hair was in a bun. No strand lingering, the puritanical cleanness of her forehead caught the sunlight. Pages of her book turned in gentle measure like a schoolmarm.

It was touching how desperately uninteresting she was trying to make herself. A blue coat with purple buttons. There was something otherworldly in her dullness, that her nun-like simplicity indicated a preoccupation with the intangible.

We developed coinciding travel routines. In the morning she wore a fierce grin while walking down the platform. Standing alone, she smiled in a light of unknown source. One evening as I walked home she skipped down the sidewalk, her white rabbit feet sneakers cycling a heartbeat. It froze me. Childlike madness in widow-like attire.

I've made a habit of fantasizing about the most boring woman in the world. That in truth she is wicked and heartless, that her tasteless clothing is how she punishes herself for a compulsion to hurt others. That she is some kind of witch. Her attire is a shield, their conservatism impenetrable. Every curve of her body flattened, the warmth of her cheeks neutralized. I imagine she smells like bar soap.

It gives me great joy to invent scenes of satanic torment in her private life. Hissing through gapped teeth as hot wax drips on her pearly toes. The monkeyish determination in her face as she devours a rodent.

My wife says I tend to ascribe depth where there is none. That sometimes people are as they appear.

Too many people on the train Monday. Pressed arm to arm, sitting, standing. There was one seat open. I didn't see coffee spilled on it, no baby around, so I took it. A treat! I realized the most boring woman in the world sat before me. I was her captive.

Nausea bloomed in my jaws and it terrified me how readily all my visions set upon me. That all my academic leanings, my questing in novels, that my fascination with her dullness was a longing to break the blank isolation of my life. That she could be the myth to splinter the spiritual order. I've come to shelter religious objects, fantasies of persons I can never possess. This nameless tasteless woman was my paraphilic love map, my great unending flaw. A keen interest in destroying myself.

A purple button on her blue coat was missing. A duffle bag lay between her sneakers. A big dirty white blanket was bundled in her lap. She clutched the blanket, her grip tightening with every bump. Her hands were chapped like little red claws. This touched me, her thoughtlessness to her own wellbeing. She beamed a smile at me that made me feel like a warm little lump of sugar. I followed her home and learned where she lived.

She lived two blocks past the park. I could've had a drink anywhere. But I chose a bar across the street from her apartment. After four drinks, how did I expect myself not to go near it?

At first, I just stared at it. Smoking. The shutters liver purple. It was the shabbiest building on the block. Mottled brick. How did I expect myself not to go near it?

At first, I sat on the stoop.

At first, I rang the doorbell. A little white candy. A couple jabs. Then I leaned in. Then I smashed my knuckles at it a dozen times. I tried the locked door. I banged on the glass. The longer I waited the more persistent I became. A man came down the hall and looked at me. I kept smacking the glass. He let me in. I apologized.

It looked like an old Victorian boarding house. Somber dark walls, long red carpet. The banister thick and dry under my hand.

I knocked on the door. Then hid. Then knocked. Then hid. No answer. I stepped back and stared at the door with a wounded gaze, like that peephole was her eye and I wanted her to witness my crumpled drunk posture. To disturb her, to gape at me like a zoo animal, clutching that ugly blue coat with those chapped hands.

The next morning, I lived in terror of being confronted. I imagined her face twisting in ridicule, her words curling with hatred and people looking on. That she would insult me, shove me and shout. That I wouldn't take the challenge, I would be cleansed by fire. Degrade me until I can love it.

But she smiled at me and I realized she knew nothing.

That as I stood in that hallway the night before, aching and drunk, she probably had ear phones on, or was showering, or sleeping. I was not permitted to share my madness with her.

I've become friends with the most boring woman in the world. We first started talking on the train platform. Earlier that morning I had been sorting boxes. I was helping my wife move out. I was sorting boxes. Fitting boxes into boxes. And I started to think about all the things in life we keep in boxes. Emotions, memories, failed relationships, fears. We put boxes in boxes in boxes. And one day, if you're lucky, you get put in a box. Then I started to lose myself. The boxes started to disintegrate.

That night I went to that bar across the street from her apartment. It was loud and crowded with people younger than me, I was intimidated. A lot of young professionals with notepads and big glasses, crossing their arms at each other. I sat near the dartboard. The waiter wanted to know if I was alright but backed off when I ordered a drink. It became an experiment, sitting there alone, unsure of myself and drinking, chronicling every detail.

The rest goes in and out. I remember grappling with blocks of sidewalk, looking over my shoulder, being grateful the weather wasn't too cold. A tall thin black man with dreads down his back stood on the corner. Handsome in a somber way with a case of rings he made from spoons. I'd seen him many times before in the daylight. I approached him and he gave me a ring. All I remember is I started to cry. I couldn't stop and I kept apologizing. Strangers were looking at me and then pretending not to look at me. I remember trying to hold hands with the black man, that I wanted some companionship. He started to tell me about a girlfriend or a sister or a mother that was hit by a train but I couldn't listen. He smelled like stale unwashed skin. He kept telling me he would pray for me. This upset me even more. He was stopped by a policeman and I fled.

Made it to the big stone pillared department store. Leaned into the showcase with these mannequins, smooth heads like black eggs, hands like sharp fins curled at their waists. I felt a hand on my arm.

I was discovered by the most boring woman in the world. With that strange talent she has of materializing without footsteps, a hovering hallucination. She levelled me with those intent brown eyes. Take me in. Make me your hostage.

"What are you doing here?" I asked her because I didn't know what to say, trying to inform the silence. She did not answer. I marveled at her icy ability to detach from present situations. When the most boring woman in the world did not answer me, I was consumed with rage. To feel so directionless, helpless, ignored, felt like a crime against myself. That her cruel ambivalence, her disinterest in her wardrobe or any outward expression of personality, terrified me. I could not break her. She made me question myself, what I thought I deserved, my egotism. In response I adopted a posture of submission, that to somehow submit would bring me a godly calm. A greater understanding. My tenderness for her was curdling. She touched my arm, the shock of her hand terrified me. The surging pressure of meeting flesh. My wife was calling me.

"Aren't you going to get that?" she asked.

I've made a lover of the most boring woman in the world. She is the terror I imagined. Her body is an unspeakable wonder. There's a scar from aged fifteen and I can picture it so clearly. Back pack slumped by the toilet, door locked, mirror fogged. The razor. Another scar. Cigarette burn on the inside of her arm, a purple bullseye. Another scar, stitches in her fingers after she slammed them in a car door.

"You never ask me questions about myself" she said one day when we were naked. I wanted her to shame me for this. Every crack of the paddle took my breath away. I've theorized the pain, likened it to impulses of aggression in primates, likened it to biblical proportion. I have given undue burden to the most boring woman in the world. I place my life in her hands. With every rip at my skin, she reminds me that with her care for atmosphere, dark rooms and black clothing, that under my salary and my marriage, I am a beast. She quarters my muscles on a metal table and dines on me. Her unrelenting questions like scalpels, I answer aloud my greatest wish.

One evening she refused me. I pinned her hair to the floor with my boot. I recognized a deepening fear that this would be the last time we saw each other. And as I looked down at her, bright eyes horrified, I knew how weak she truly was. A small unnamed woman with filthy habits.

When my lawyer requested her testimony, she resumed her nun-like attire, as though I had never touched her. It broke me how hard she tried not to look at me. Like I was some ugly little dog tied to a parking meter. I've made a habit of forgetting the most boring woman in the world. That as I sit on my cot and remove my shoes, her face isn't resting on the cement floor, chin tilted back as I entered her. The vague sickness of that longing does not leave. It transformed into a sweet perversion, to make myself invisible. And if I close my eyes, if I ignore how hard it is to breathe, I am in that place again. She's putting on the band aids and I don't feel it. My suffering has meant nothing. It's already over.

Mother in the Tower

Her mother cried because she bought the tickets. Big movie, brought the kid along. They read about it in the paper, lines around the block. The sort of thing you saw so you could talk about it real loud at the barbecue. Wedge of potato wiggling in the corner of your mouth, oh yes, I saw that one last week. That one scene where all their bikes lifted off the ground. Came to tears, believe me, just tears.

Her mother cried because she bought the tickets, not a sentimental woman though. But maybe something about this movie, the teenagers and their anxiety, all working together, the unrelenting determination of their sneakers on bike pedals, sweating, heaving with sirens behind them. Their whole lives just our collective moment, running from judgment and the pursuit of broader powers. And they're just about to give in, escalating pulses, megaphones screeching, and when hope is sneaking out that dim little aperture, they lift off. They're free when they least expected it.

The daughter took her son, who as a grown man wouldn't remember any of it. Half way through the movie, daughter wiping her face, the mother said, "Don't you think this is kind of corny?"

But the daughter wasn't there anymore. Movies had that effect, sit in the seat and look up and all those little things didn't exist anymore. The broken toaster. Her husband's car keys by an empty soda can. The daughter could still dream.

But the mother had trouble earlier in the week. Cops involved, practically a local celebrity. If you steal a piece of furniture, hardly anyone suspects you. You're on your way out the store, moving a vanilla leather recliner at glacial pace. How could anybody steal such a big thing? But that's what the mother was, always eyes on big things. Once the love of a boy at seventeen, then the love of her brother-in-law. Maybe this is where the daughter got it.

When the movie ended they hobbled onto the sidewalk and the mother lit a cigarette. The little boy was tired and wanted to go home. The daughter looked ahead, pretending she hadn't heard him. She didn't want to leave the theater yet, people dropping candy wrappers and laughing. What was home? Her husband slapping the dirt out of his glove on the kitchen counter? Maybe that sad way he looked at her when she tried to tell him she wanted more, she was smart enough for more. He'd listen for about thirty more years. Then out of sight. Like those kids on their bikes in the movie.

And when the mother read the daughter her tarot that night something ugly looked back at them. All the daughter understood was the small blonde woman depicted on the card, plunging headlong out a window. The Tower. The woman's hair fanned around her shoulders, socket-shock frizzy in free fall. Out the window, her blue robes fluttering. Change, the mother assured her, don't let the silly pictures get to you. But like the frames of the film earlier, the tarot card imprinted itself in the daughter's mind. Smoking in bed with her son asleep, a gray worm of ash fell in her lap and she didn't even notice. The Tower was on fire and they were jumping out the window to save themselves.

The mother dreamt about her first love that night. Seventeen, just a boy down the street. It's not like something tragic happened to him, he didn't die, just moved away. Right after the storm came through in '38. Most of them drowned, some sucked up in the sky. The town smelled so bad after the storm. But the mother and this boy were in love and fucked before the storm. They thought it would be their last chance to know anything real before dying. Just as good a story as any, that this was it and they may not make it to their twenties. Their parents were ravaging the market, packing deck chairs in sheds, taking drugs to be quiet. Fifty some odd years later, the mother lay in bed and dreamt about the boy. Skinny and tall, never her type afterward. He was talking but she couldn't make out the words. Then he did it. Pinched his belly button like a zipper and unzipped his whole body. Nothing but light. No organs or intestines inside like the kind they'd seen dangling from trees after the storm. The boy was light and she thought maybe this was like when Moses saw the back of God, that God kept their real face from him so they wouldn't have to kill him.

And the little son woke up before the sunrise, he was dreaming ET was chasing him. But ET wasn't tender and funny, his feet made that wet slapping noise on the kitchen tiles and he growled like he was hungry. So hungry for little boy flesh. The little boy woke up but his mother next to him did not. She did not move. She was pretending to sleep. So, the little boy got out of the bed and out of the room, looking in on grandma for a minute. Her breasts were flat on her belly in her thin white nightgown like two wallets. The son went to the kitchen to play with the stove.

The flames weren't like the ones in the cartoons, these were short and blue, not raving red tongues climbing as tall as his father. And that smell of gas, his small fingers twitching inches over the burner. The son jumped when he heard the knocks. Hard and fast, like somebody who needed help. And the face on the other side of the window was ghost gray like a film negative. The son thought to get help but didn't want to get in trouble for playing with the stove. So, he took it upon himself. No father around, he had to guard the women.

The mother got up when she noticed her son was gone too long. Up to no good just like his mother. Knocked on his back, kitchen door wide open, she thought he was having a seizure. His limbs going wild like a fish on the deck of a boat. And when she stepped back to measure her breaths, her gleaming brown eyes widened on the glowing burner. Fire. A foot of air around the stove was thick with heat, knob warm.

He couldn't tell his mother or grandmother just what he saw. No glass was broken so he must've let them in. Whoever he let in. But nothing was missing. No furniture knocked over, no mud on the floor. It had been raining after all, this heat wave couldn't last forever. Don't you tell me about those spaceships, the mother told the son when he tried to speak. It was that movie, the grandma told her daughter. And maybe this intricate fairy tale the boy was trying to convey was something like what his adults conducted. Distorted reconstructions of the past to escape ordinary self-awareness. But it's true, and the tears went down his cheeks. And the shaking hands stopped, his lips tightened with rage. The fever subsided.

After the boy went to sleep, the mother and daughter sat at the kitchen table drinking. It was her husband's whiskey. They wanted to drink it so he wouldn't, not at home in front of the boy. And the daughter told the mother she was pregnant again. And the daughter wished the kitchen was burning down with them inside.

Planes don't fly this low in these parts, thought the mother when a loud noise descended on their conversation and the house began to shake. The pepper shaker fell off the counter and broke. The little boy was awake in the doorway, taking this very moment to announce that he'd been right all along. And the daughter started to worry, that what if these were aliens and she was pregnant with some alien-human hybrid they'd implanted in her cervix while hypnotized by talk shows. And the mother regretted buying the tickets for that movie and worse, crying at the movie. But worst of all, she regretted the white bird's eye maple chairs she once stole that they sat on that made the worst scratching noise on the floor every time you moved.

Then there was the dog. She stopped greeting people when her hips went but when the house started shaking and the silverware rattled in the drawers and the pictures fell off the wall, she bolted from the carpet like she was young and ready. Her husky old barks, she had a mouth on her like all the other women in the house.

The boy tried to grab the dog and in fright she bit him. She'd never done this before, the boy stumbled back crying and the mother grabbed the dog's collar and pulled her into the other room as the daughter consoled her son. The dog gave a picture to the mother in its eyes, like it knew there was something awry, as if to tell her, you dumb old lady, you didn't have the nerve to read your own tarot tonight.

It stopped. The daughter holding the son, the mother holding the dog. Different rooms, all waiting, breathless and relieved. A car alarm shrieked outside. When the mother went out to check for her car, it was no longer there. Just a scorched stretch of earth, big as a grave. But the mother didn't care too much, she'd stolen that too.

The Price of Love

I bought her to love me. Those plastic capped eyes saw right through me. The shoulder length brown hair, just like my daughter. But we don't speak anymore so maybe she's done what the others girls do. To her hair. Go green. Pierce their faces. But my lover wouldn't do that. The transaction is never acknowledged, like a covert adoption. She could have arrived in my living room by straw basket, malevolent tides, as if the forces that compelled us together would consent to destroy us. Just because I purchased her does not mean she is powerless. I've grown my suspicions of her.

Small behavioral displays increasingly atypical and frequent. A sharp reply. Faltering eye contact.

Sometimes I think she hates for me to touch her. She sits silent before the window long hours. When I first took her in our house, her steady gaze inventoried every detail. The metal handle hanging off the dresser. A chipped tile on the bathroom floor. A mouse trap behind the stove. My imperfections charmed her, my large insectile eyes and paper cuts. The way I smile to hide my poor teeth. Maybe she was stringing all these flaws together like pearls. Anal beads.

It took time to get used to her skin. But if I closed my eyes it was just like mine.

Her speech is changing. Sometimes she doesn't finish sentences. The narrowness of this house has given freedom to disobedient thoughts. Her isolation makes her resent me.

One morning she was lining up knives on the kitchen table and smiling. She said it was a message from my daughter. That was the first time I turned her off. I called the company and explained her actions, they offered to send out a representative. This suggestion was ignored.

In bed last night she choked me. I wonder if she was hacked.

Apollo's Chapel

Moonbeam was nineteen from Ohio, reared in a modest upbringing of Polish immigrants who worked in the steel mill outside Cincinnati. She dropped out of school in the tenth grade to pursue ballet on the roof and have tea parties with a neighbor boy across the street with a blotchy birthmark under his left eye. One night Moonbeam gathered her clothes in a lettuce colored bed sheet and tied it with a white stocking. She crept down the stairs and out the door. Her only luggage aside from a sack was fifteen dollars and a calf-skin bound journal her grandmother in Montreal sent her last Christmas.

Hitchhiking to Omaha, she caught a ride with a trucker transporting bales of hay to the Utah Border, fragments of straw blowing in the plumes of exhaust from the tailpipe, decorating the interstate. She fell asleep against the window, jets of steam lingering under her nostrils as her tortoise shell rimmed glasses knocked on the glass, adorned in a vignette of frost.

Once in Nevada she kindles a friendship with an old woman on a ranch who offered her room and board at a price of her labors. Moonbeam awoke one morning with the old woman hovering over her with a teapot, muttering curses about the hippie movement, crater from her body still deep in the sofa. She left all her belongings back at that ranch, including the journal from grandma. Moonbeam contemplated returning to the ranch to slaughter the old woman and remove her belongings but instead she never got around to it. Instead she accepted the loss of her belongings, the remaining prospects of her home in Ohio, and lived again alone and dispossessed.

She came to Apollo's Chapel in the Spring of '65, walking barefoot through the prairie, clutching her arms and singing an ancient riddle about stars. She hadn't eaten in three days and could feel herself emaciated, knobby knees knocking against the grains. The area was a pig farm before it was seized by the IRS. After that it was abandoned, until Viracocha, a muralist from Monterey, migrated thirty miles north of the California border, and pitched a tent establishing his commune of Apollo's Chapel. He protested the local farmers by lodging his feces in their mailboxes. They all came at him one day, the farmers brought their sons and made them stand by the trucks and watch as men flogged him. After that beating they left him alone, discarding the patch of rural Oregon to Viracocha.

Viracocha wrote letters to his friends in the San Fran and Bodega Bay, encouraging the fleets of bohemians to join his commune. He was building a religion, and when he saw Moonbeam while stoking a flame with his elbows capped in soot, he clutched his member thick as a swan neck and called for the children of the camp. He opened his arms to her, constructed a bed of reeds for her to sleep on, and painted her shoulders in blue dyes. Moonbeam felt honored to be his mural, she was adopted by the commune and the women bathed her in suds of Rosemary and palm oil, sponging her ankles and cackling with joy. At dusk she smoked from a glass cylinder and made love to the men and women around the log pupil Viracocha arranged, where he watched with pride as he leaned on a staff carved from white poplars, huffing a Native prayer dedicated to the Klamath tribe who inhabited these parts for ten thousand years.

She fashioned shell necklaces for all the women and played flutes carved from cedar and river cane. They sat under a tarp that sunk with rain, devouring camas bulbs that taste like sweet potatoes. In the morning the women picked wild strawberries, their naked white bodies flashing through the fields, dandelions tucked behind their ears and their wrists bound in sunlight.

Moonbeam was in love with a black girl named Teardrop. Teardrop was from Houston before she converted to nature's nymphets. Moonbeam was seduced by her kindness, her innocent politeness. As a gift, Teardrop sewed Moonbeam moccasins from her sundress, which Moonbeam never wore but perched on her pillow and kissed before she dreamt. Their tongues tingled with acid on the flat rocks in the water, worn smooth with a gray austerity. Eddies swirling, mystified by this aquatic tangent in the meadow. Their pupils doubled in diameter as they hugged each other naked in the stream, Coho salmon tickling their calves.

A man named Footprint arrived at the commune a month after Moonbeam, he was a vet from Nam and asked Viracocha to extinguish the demons from his soul, to which they purgatoried their torsos and thanked the constellations for their union. Teardrop married Moonbeam under a willow. Viracocha provided the rings, made from the flexible stems of a plant, tied in a knot around their fingers. The men captured sparrows at noon and threw them in the air when they kissed, the night was filled with peyote sanctity and speaking caverns in the grove. Moonbeam caressed the inky coiled vines of Teardrop's tresses, pressing her long brown skin with flower petals. A doe wandered across their tent in the morning, and both interpreted this as earth's fertility for blessings.

Peace has been found in Apollo's Chapel. The commune rejoiced in their existence, fornicating before the smoldering altars of their convictions. Repulsed by the subtle ruin of decimals and dollar signs; repulsed by a society that composed a shield of morals, declaring right and wrong like items in a supermarket. Could their televisions tell them what real love was? Could their radiators and rockets warm their capitalist hearts? Did the sun ever settle on their sternums and proclaim it loved them? They knew nothing of peace, they knew nothing of spirituality. Apollo's Chapel was Eden, preserved in folly and skylines.

One afternoon, Moonbeam returned from the forest after gathering ferns for a meditation mat. She stumbled into a tent, glowing with torches from burning tree branches. The people surrounded Viracocha, kneeling before a goose slit open with its intestines dangling above the soil. They were chanting, pounding their fists in their thighs and mournfully raising their bloodshot eyes. The ritual was proceeding undisturbed by Moonbeam's presence. Teardrop was praying too, her purple lips blowing air on the nape of Footprint's neck. Moonbeam ran from the tent, distraught by their pagan endeavors, stung with confusion and fear.

Moonbeam was going to leave Apollo's Chap. The commune was no longer a habitat for hallucinogens but a dedication to idolatry. Nature was supposed to be their god. The wind and the mountains were their disciples, their bible was a strip of bark and their rosary was a daffodil. What was this business with the dissected fowl? Viracocha, their blue-eyed prophet, led this vessel into an absolution of slaughtered animals.

Teardrop encountered Moonbeam outside their tent with her moccasins in hand. She could sense Moonbeam's panic to Viracocha's practices and embraced her with reason and sympathy.

"We are honoring Nature, Moonbeam, that goose you saw was a precious child of nature like you and I. Please, do not leave me. I love you. Take my hand" She said, reaching for Moonbeam's hands still clenching the moccasins. "I'll take you to our tent. Worship with me. Bless the animals and plants with me. Viracocha will look fondly upon your return."

Moonbeam was hesitant but her love for Teardrop overwhelmed her doubts and dismay. Moonbeam would have worshipped a leather shoe if Teardrop was there with her. Together they walked back to the tent, enveloped in smoke from the torches. Eventually Moonbeam found herself muttering the verses too, humming along to the crowd circling the goose. Viracocha placed his hand on Moonbeam's hair, a paternal disease with a taste for Ohio high school drop-outs with Ashkenazi ancestry. He placed his mouth on her ear and whispered a passage from his service. She could feel his voice rumbling in her skull and Teardrop squeezed her buttocks.

After a momentary pause, Viracocha threw the goose in the fire and clapped his hands together in finality, the way a conductor might lower his head and hands to a staff of Vivaldi.

"Thank you, my children of Apollo's Chapel. You all live inside my heart and I will die a happy hero to our salvation. We are all capable of compassion, as you have proven to me this day. Follow me to the stream where I shall bless the pebbly sand and praise our deity."

The members filtered out of the tent and held hands while crossing the pasture. They trailed behind Viracocha who cloaked himself in a sheath of moss, sewn by the chapped hands of Teardrop. Moonbeam sat on the banks of the stream, the same water that once ran through her legs as she cradled Teardrop the first time.

"Beloved stream pulsing with beauty! Bathe our faces in your unborn silence, close our minds to the rage and ruin feasting on the flesh of our dear boys in Nam. Let the light of your sanctuary blind the greedy heifers in Washington and may the music of your bursting tides sooth our ailing wisdoms."

Everyone cheered and Viracocha removed his sheath of moss from his shoulder, stepping into the stream and crying to the poplars. Moonbeam felt her hands go numb with affection as she joined Viracocha in the stream. Their backs were slick with mud and the choir of their enchantment resounded in the brush. Holy stream, their misplaced Ganges, softly trembling in their spines, prowess of an amphibious goddess, unchanging and divine.

Moonbeam attended Viracocha's services with Teardrop every evening, becoming more devout and impassioned than her contemporaries. She threw her hands above her head, spastic and entranced by the fiery climb into heaven. Her commitment was thrilling to Viracocha and he asked the commune to be more like her. She prepared the torches and helped Teardrop sew Viracocha's clothing. She whispered his prayers before she slept and when she awoke. Meaning had been restored. Sacred botany, clove and orchard, viral, timeless, pantomime and squalor. Dirty gray nails and smoke-stained cheeks, relishing in the solitude.

The last week of August, Moonbeam entered Viracocha's tent. Her hair was draped over her breasts and a bouquet of lilies fell to the ground.

"I want to be your sacrifice" she said, "I want you to offer me to our God, I am ready to give myself. My body is prepared for its eclipse."

Viracocha sat up from his cot, shifting his posture and straightening a row of cigarettes on his pillow.

"Are you sure, Moonbeam, my child? Are you truly ready to be sacrificed?" he said, fingering his naval encrusted in coffee bean colored alfalfa springs of hair.

"I want to join our God. My time on earth has been spent in vain if I cannot fulfill his duty."

"Is your wife, Teardrop, aware of this decision?"

"I have told her and she stands by me"

Viracocha was quiet for a moment, pondering the method of sacrifice to use, until he responded with a date and time.

"Tomorrow, my child, at dawn, eternity will swallow you."

Moonbeam nodded and knelt to Viracocha where she kissed his pelvis and repeated his verse. He smiled back and two cigarettes rolled off his pillow.

Dawn, a fog veiled the prairie and Teardrop sobbed in Moonbeam's hair. They left their tent and joined the crowd in Viracocha's tent. The women walked up to the altar, and stood before the congregation, their faces solemn and passive.

"My believers! Daughter Moonbeam is offering the ultimate gift to Nature, her own mortal flesh."

There were several gasps but no one interjected, instead choosing to follow Viracocha and Moonbeam out of the tent to the stream. The water was icy and opaque, but Teardrop came forward with a blanket she had sewn the previous day, multiple squares for pockets decorating the front. She placed it over Moonbeam's stomach and chest, where one by one the members of Apollo's Chapel came forward with a stone, where they placed it in a pocket on her blanket. Eventually there were forty stones and the blanket was tearing with the weight, but Moonbeam kept it pinned to her diaphragm, closing her eyes before she sunk beneath the water, beneath the weight of the stones, to drown in her faith.

They watched as Moonbeam lay flat on the bed of the stream, the water rushing over her in a crescendo of atoms and spiders. Several bubbles rose to the surface before Moonbeam's face grew pale and her mouth opened, filling with water. Her weighted corpse started from under the water like an apparition, and Teardrop sang a hymn for the stream. Footprint and Viracocha were silently groping each other behind a tree, and the members of Apollo's Chapel dispersed in the woods. The snakes buried in the soil and an owl perched on a fallen tree. The miracle of morning was frosty and faded, shrouded in mist, beckoning the watery sepulcher of Moonbeam.

Profound Desire

I've torn my maps up. That's how long they've been crunched into bloody palm rags like a monk's burning parchment. The vast obtrusive intricacies in terrain, sloping deflections of rotten cottage desolation. I have been all over the entire world, looking for my single species of intrigue. The flower, it's Latin christening: *votum profundus*, it's English neutering: *profound desire*. My first inkling of Profound Desire's existence came from the pages of a horticultural catalogue. A specific and passive section was devoted to the flower. The writer notes, "Profound Desire is a plant of rarest breed...only seen during two separate expeditions in two separate continents. The media has famously branded this plant with characteristics of revelation and psychic powers if ingested." (*LX Croupier's Encyclopedia, Vol. C, pp. 88*).

After thorough, exhausting, and conclusively despairing research, I learned that nobody on earth had seen a bouquet of Profound Desire in forty years. I was claimed to be extinct, and to my dribbling sobs, I vowed to find the flower, extract the deified harmonies from its stem and let the world know that this plant still thrived. It sprung from the earth and loomed wet and dreaming like a lover in rain, somewhere in the safaris and swamps. Dwelling in the faceless darkness of a ravine formlessly angelic, just for me.

Profound Desire has been sought by my ambitious clutches for thirty years now. I have snorted the chalk vestiges of my longing. Inquired the fragmentary polygons of countries, damned with the names of despicable sovereigns. I have married the stainless vault of my nomadic melancholy, grinning travesty of garden legend and barbed sneers deriding my efforts. I drove myself into my expedition and left myself no form of retreat.

Slashed the vines of Amazon inferno, buried my hands in the spinach viridian tides of rivers. Catapulted my arthritic knees up fatal inclines. Shattered the coiling reflections of the moon in puddles with my words dripping out sensitive anticipation. Exploiting an application for greater truth, the journey was no longer about the flower. It was no longer about my destination, the product of my labor and accretions of a nether reality. It was about my ability to pluck any whim for my attainment. My thorned challis, my nebulous pleasure implanted in my eye, coaxed from the platinum fortress of dreams.

Many, confronted with the immeasurable fears of failure, would not have spared three decades of their lives to find Profound Desire, but I did. Instead of retracting in uncertainty, I drank. Sometimes I ponder my existence if I'd had a family, but my independence is alienating and I'm too selfish to change.

In the night I carve out my heart with images of savoring the iridescent petals of Profound Desire with the bleached oyster of my tongue. Unfledged and ineffectual, I simmer in petty delicacies of though. Limping and irregular, I crush my hands against the mirrors. All are disguised with one final name, a single foe in my tingled spasm, titled Profound. Repeat after me, Profound. Profound. Profound. Profound. Profanely, profusely, and preferably Profound. Profound. Profound, your first name, the swooning pout of your mother's snarled harmony. Entangling inconclusive violation, Desire. Desire. Your surname, a vermillion treachery of primitive and hypnotizing contradiction.

So, it has come to this? There remain no shreds of paradise. I'm sinking faster than I can comprehend. When I catch my identical cadaver in the shaft of my knife, I am stunned. Expressionless but tumescent. Belching an apology because I've got no remorse.

The other night I had a dream, the most awful love of my life came to me. I dreamt that I became a scabby and saggy old man after all my terrible lonely expeditions that mocked me with failure, I returned home. Home, it was a place I'd never seen before with all the furniture and draping of a film set before dismantled. All perfect. All serene. Hobbling across the carpet with my Velcro sneakers shuffling the dullest cough of static.

My suitcase on the ground and my barnacled hands curling around a bathroom door knob. Being old, I panicked at my aching groin and inflexible thin legs. Inside the toilet, sprouted from holy urine stains and shadowy molds encrusted under the seat. Votum Profundus, silk thorn in my heart. My love. Profound Desire in my toilet and my trembling valves choked on ecstasy.

My declining body lunged at the toilet and in mid-spring, became young and colorful. I was younger than the man I am today. I threw my meaty palms around the stem and ripped my desire from the toilet like pulling a tendril from a maiden's scalp. I bled seedlings of joy and gorged myself in the most disgusting greatness. Opened my eyes and the stench was unbearable. My hands once throbbing and genuine softened into the claws of an old man. Profound Desire was absent, my hands were covered with feces from the toilet and my mouth was black and pasty.

You can only imagine my waking in a cot under the swelling canopy of my tent, sunken with rain and slick perspiring neck gasping. Mosquitoes feasting upon me in my frightening blindness. The true parasite is that which goes unnoticed until it poisons its prey. My life is spent spinning from continent to continent. Rising with the same expectations and recoiling to my bed in defeat after hours have evaporated in their same cruel persuasion. All endeavors of realistic virtue have deserted me. My only child and heir are Profound Desire, carrying my name and blood in its dilated wonder.

How did I proceed? What truth could I ordain without any coins of attainment? Did I know anything except the shivering flowered hexagon I cradled behind my eyes because there was nothing more relieving? This is my orchestra, my wedding, my history, my fidelity. All control of the situation is handled. I'm not as strange as I appear. I'm worse.

I reached the tip of Afraid and vowed it was the end. Vowed to divorce my madness and die alone in poverty. Nobody would want to hire a man of my age, nor do I possess the resources or relatives to postpone this inevitability. I decided I would rather live as a failure than a craving insomniac. This revelation was spawned in the tip of Africa where the air is a hotly blurred purgatory of animal shit in the streets that leaves me vulgar and bitter. The burnt taste of smoke in my mouth with all the words that never meant anything.

Soon I took to the jungle, slept in the trees and bathed in prehistoric rain. A spider bite above my tailbone like an itching walnut. I feast on turtles, fish, and small birds. I have retained a combat knife from my youth and it has served me well. I live in the crude modesty of savage filth. My only fears revolve around starvation and snakes. Any particular passion has been starved and muffled in my sleep. Again, in that sincere pathetic way, the sort of way that can be gazed on with pity by ignorant scorn.

An evening occurred where I dined on a snail at the base of a tree and nourished my isolation briefly. A shade in my periphery, quietly waiting for my acknowledgement, bowed to the soil and I to it. At last, is it truly you? My period on earth was devoted to you, and now you are not the faintest character in my scheme. You appear at my feet with your fever of silence, like an estranged spouse. I am old, but you, votum profundus, you are still young. You haven't missed me at all.

I buried you because I couldn't stand looking at you. Then I dug you up and ate you. My canines slit your palms. You tasted like soapy vinegar and silk. Tore your green spiked spine as my fingers dripped red on my chin. My tongue was sore and swollen, my breathing slowed. I waited, mesmerized and obedient to my wish. The poison got me. Profound Desire tinged my bloodstream and sent it missionaries all over my body to save me. My final minute was an emergency of will, I forfeited to my alembic hallucination. Profound Desire, poisoning my potential and intoxicating my logic. Thank you for finding me, I close my eyes and forget about you.

Casino Tom

Casino Tom briefly lived above the Riviera Tango on the boulevard with all the Trump hotels glittering in their acid baths of neon hyperbole, calling out in the darkness like a blind rat in the sewer of dismay. Acropolis abound with whores and pow wows with the maître de boss of basement blowjobs, quarter in the naval and kneecap on the shoulder. Casino Tom was full of apparitions, memories he thought he left back east to the chimney on the chapel melted with the craniums of children, boiling down some vague freedom that lasted as long as the whiskey might have if Casino Tom had any self-control.

Casino Tom came out west because he got into a scuffle with his girlfriend in the trailer park. She was screaming something about his lack of commitment, witnessed in the dust diners scattered along the interstate with some Anglo-Irish snowflake in braids and an apron. His girlfriend picked up the shot glasses from the cupboard and continued to hurl them at the screen door, shattered glass splintering down the rusted frame as Casino Tom wrung his hands, explaining his misbehaviors as a result of her inability to orgasm and their estrogen complexities. He meant to be a good person but it's just so damn hard to please anybody.

He slapped her down on the gravel and pointed to the pubescent mothers standing outside their trailers, craning their necks over their mailboxes with a red infant on their hips, oozing feces and sobbing uncontrollably. The faces of fathers under the brim of their white baseball caps twitched in stubbled fury, insisting to their wives in whispers that the Luger lived in the drawer beside the cheese grater.

Casino Tom went out west and spent some time in El Paso and Albuquerque, sleeping on Greyhounds that sailed through the night like submarines into the void, headlights bouncing down the slick road no longer parched for a Midwestern rain. Vegas was the spotlight in the desert that glimmered and sand through the stars, hovering invisibly in a cloud of exhaust and elation, stinking like a butane bomb waiting for his flicker. The indefinite possibility of life outside the trailer park struck some fear he had not subdued. Away from ma and pa's ranch, populated by domesticated animals that replaced him and his siblings they left to live alone; guinea pig stool behind the piano bench and yellow feather clinging to the sofa.

He thought Vegas was full of freaks in tiaras, pimps in paper blue lapels, and showgirls gone sour in the nunnery of the crack house, offering their sequined bikinis in exchange for a distraction, smoking fairy dust to assuage some homeless irony skittering through the walls. It was just an electric factory palpitating with midnight guilt, running from taxi and down the sidewalk like children at a parade, acknowledging a hangover as a dismal price for salvation.

Three weeks in the city and Casino Tom was evicted from his apartment above the Riviera Tango. The landlord was some pimpled Austrian whose shiny scalp glistening in Rogaine and stank like the cheap cologne they sold at the five and dime with some French name to rebuke its lack of sophistication. He must have thought he smelled like a sultan in that bottled filth. He was just a perfumed rat in overalls with no sympathy for Casino Tom.

Evicted and broke, Casino Tom slept in the doorway of the projector palace that exhibited Swedish skin flicks in the evenings. The security guard spotted him and smacked his shoulder with a rolled-up newspaper, spitting purple phlegm in the gutter. Casino Tom snatched the newspaper from the guard and waved it ferociously at the key ring jangling on his belt, smiting the guard with his elemental anguish and blue-collar bias against authority.

After being chased from the porn house, Casino Tom settled on the curb in front of the Filipino cuisine and opened the newspaper to the wanted ads. One ad caught his attention, an ad from a Miss Iowa Davies, seeking a driver. Casino Tom tore out the column and headed towards a payphone, panhandling near a fountain, sustaining his nausea with their infrared bulbs glowing under the foamy water. Two tourists gave him a dollar in change and Casino Tom thanked them profusely for their donation to his destitution. Finding a payphone, he sealed himself up in the glass cubicle and called Miss Iowa Davies.

The woman who answered the phone must have been a dinosaur because Casino Tom had to repeat everything he said three times and spelled his names at least twice. She seemed to like him, though, there was a naive eagerness in her old vocal chords and Casino Tom thought this might have been a mistake.

"You've got the job" she said

"But you haven't met me yet" Tom muttered in his palm.

"We'll fix that. Come to my house in the morning and we'll start tomorrow.

The old woman recited her address to Casino Tom with slow deliberate pride, whether she was proud of the address or her ability to remember the address is unknown. She seemed like some spinster with a load of cash she was looking to flush through some coward's veins. He briefly questioned the authenticity of the interview; its brevity was like a glance, swift and heavy with unspoken prospects.

I got the job I got the job, Casino Tom repeated in disbelief at the gray shred of the newspaper pinned between his thumb and forefinger, trembling in the wind like a gust of ominous mythology his hickbilly brain could not comprehend. His hunger defeated his skepticism.

Casino Tom hitchhiked a ride to Iowa Davie's estate, a Victorian wart in a cul-de-sac, emanating a medieval disdain from its stony foyer. He got there at ten in the morning and Iowa Davies was finishing the translation of some Hindi text for a museum. The house was filled with porcelain figurines of children scooping water from wells and embracing lambs. There was a painting in the hallway of the crucifixion and an Abyssian feline slinked across the molding. When he entered the study of Iowa Davies, the windows had been opens and a lizard sat on the sill.

"Tom, sit down, son." Iowa Davies' mouth was a chapped slat like an incision in her face, widening with words about wages and weekdays. She seemed nice enough and did not succumb to senility like Casino Tom had imagined. When Casino Tom stood from his chair to shake her hand, she pulled out from behind the desk and came forward in a wheelchair, the metal spokes twinkling in the sunlight from the open window.

She steadily extended her grip to Tom, who took it quickly, trying to hide his surprise. They worked out a schedule of Saturdays through Thursdays, from ten to five. Iowa Davies offered Casino Tom three times the money he thought he would get. There was something desperate about the old woman, and Tom began to think that maybe she wasn't looking for a driver but a companion. He didn't know how to feel for that subject, but it didn't matter anyway because he was barely a friend to himself.

Casino Tom came to the estate of Iowa Davies six days a week and she always served him lunch and dinner. She even bought him some new clothes and this intensified his discomfort. He started to go to the barber Iowa Davies recommended, and she polished him into a chauffeur of a bygone era. Replying yes ma'am and no ma'am.

Iowa Davies would be hoisted into the backseat of the Cadillac with the teeth of her ermine cradling her shoulders and she'd talk like she was Scarlett O'Hara. Casino Tom played along because he pitied her, no children or spouse, just a wheelchair and a house full of books. Thinking about Miss Iowa Davies at her empty dinner table, the utensils small and flimsy in her hands like toys, practicing her manners on the servants, made Casino Tom quiet.

One afternoon Iowa Davies asked Casino Tom to the house, and upon his arrival he noticed that the house was silent for she had dismissed all the help for the day. He found her in the living room, sitting in front of the fireplace and talking to herself. Casino Tom was hesitant to make his presence known; she seemed to be in a private moment. But the old woman was aware, and she turned her glassy black eyes on Tom and folded her hands in her lap in a sort of conventional Catholic school obedience.

"Tom, today I want you to take me to the lake. Can you do that for me?"

"Yes ma'am. I'll get the car ready."

"Wait a minute, just sit in the hall."

"Okay, well call me when you're ready."

People were absent from the lake now that the summer past. Casino Tom lowered the window for Iowa, who stuck her hand out the window and sparsely articulated the feeling of air on her skin. Her eyes lit up with a childish glee when she saw the water, pulling back from the sandy crevices near the jetty. He smiled to himself as Iowa started to talk about when she was a kid and how she loved to swim, and that the last time she had been to this lake was when she was a child. She said she lived in a cabin two kilometers from the site, but Casino Tom had difficulty picturing her in such a poor and remote sliver of land.

"Tom," she said while placing a hand on his shoulder, "I am going to tell you something because I trust you and I know you're a good man." Iowa Davies opened her white leather handbag and removed a bulky manila envelope she handed Casino Tom. He opened and closed it immediately.

"I can't," he said.

"I know you've been down on your luck but there's enough there to get you out of this place."

Tom opened the envelope again and stared, one bottom lip pinched between his overbite.

"I am an unhappy woman, Tom. I have written a suicide note on my desk. I need you to push this car into the lake."

"I can't do that"

"Sure, you can", a gloved hand seizing the steering wheel, her voice filled with the same melancholy Casino Tom had been running away from all his life. "I need you to do this for me, help me"

Casino Tom unbuttoned his collar and sighed, clenching the wheel and watching the water, beautiful in its consistent emergence and withdrawal from the tarnished mirror of the lake.

White specks of gulls circled above the Cadillac and a wind chime on the porch of a foreclosed rowhome panged solemnly in the distance. Casino Tom looked up from the dashboard to Iowa, who held his gaze without fear or grudge.

He got out of the car, stuffed the envelope in the waistband of his trousers. He made a semicircle around the hood of the car, walking up to her window and placing a hand on the polished roof that glinted in midday sun like the metallic shell of an insect. He kicked off his shoes and began to push the car down the banks into the water. As he approached the tide he retreated to the back of the vehicle, where he strained himself through the dunes. The wheels groaned and Iowa stuck her hand out the window one final time before the car was swallowed.

Casino Tom stood on the land and watched the roof of the car disappear in the lake like the hump of a whale, back into darkness, back into nothingness, a liquid grave. He ripped open the envelope and tossed the contents to the winds, bills like paper wings floating down the sand, following a northern wind. His shoes were sitting in the sand staring back at him like two grim faces, smooth and soiled. The envelope was tumbling down the jetty towards the water and clouds had formed over the clumps of mimosas located by the dirt road.

Maybe he would head back to the desert, back to Vegas, be broke and tired trying to forget. Maybe Iowa said all those nice things to him to get him to agree with her.

She was the only person who seemed to care where Casino Tom lingered. He didn't have to feel bad for her anymore. He didn't have to be sad about it late at night in the motel with the antifreeze blue bed sheets and shells of soap decorated in pubic hair. Maybe time has a way of dissolving these sorts of things. It won't ease, it won't remember and it will always love him. His future is a case for his own discretion, and never was there a solution. Be he didn't expect one, he didn't expect a savior, and if he was rewarded with such fineries he'd doubt his own rectitude. It's been said.

Wives of Red Tunnel

If you take the bridge over the harbor, past the crooning sloppy cargo steamers and sandy banks that eat your feet in the sun, you enter my town. If you pass the crusty blue tavern near the farmhouse, pass the bridge with bleached stones, you're almost there. The town of Red Tunnel, only territory I knew enough to disdain, was my home and boyhood tragedy. Now, as a fickle wrinkly janitor in a city two states away, I know the careful, uneasy slowness in Red Tunnel better than I did as a child impaired with ambition.

In the dust at my heels sleeps Red Tunnel keeping all the things I forgot. Even though I have not returned in forty-six years, and never wish to, I still dream of Red Tunnel. I dream about the town not in fuzzy nostalgia, but with the grim fear that there is a whole lifetime inside me destroyed and misunderstood forever, and it makes me crazy in the night, the deep night when I am alone.

My parents were loving, working. How could they have known what was happening to me when I left their house? Their hands hurt in motor oil and soap but did they ever ask me if I was fine? I lied, lied as I have my entire life, without a single feasible satisfaction in sight. I liked when I was too lazy to fix myself and looked at the world expecting a change. A month before I turned eighteen, I fell into the hands of Button's Murphy.

-Buttons, that's a nice name. I complimented her in the baseball diamond across from the church the day I met her. Buttons went to my school but I never talked to her. I saw her in the halls and never looked her in the face. She was quiet and unpopular, no friends and left rooms unnoticed because she didn't have any weight in conversations. I always knew she was there but I was never that interested in her. There were other girls, prettier with bigger tits that I cared about.

Buttons often hung remote and alone but if you ever asked her where she was going, in all likelihood she was headed home. People said that

Buttons had a mother only fourteen years older, no father, and followed her daughter with the prehensile sensitivity and smothering appetite of a hawk. This overbearing blood chain sliced away every living part of Buttons until she was barely a squeaking myopic flower pinched in the corner of a classroom.

Our damp lethargic seaside town tasted like sleep and sadness in the winter evenings when the sun was only a teasing shadow in the gutter. The second time I talked to Buttons I was walking the streets before sunset, more rain was supposed to be coming. It was cold rain, that frost resurrection of rain that passes through your bones every other house like the thunderous shaking of cobblestone from the trolley. Buttons walked ahead of me and stopped at the street lamp to stand in the orange island of light, clutching her ash blue raincoat. Moths waltzed from her elbows like snowflakes and she dropped her stained and checkered hand sewn purse when she saw me.

-What are you doing out here in this terrible weather? I asked her, smiling like a sun that relieved her shy heart. She retracted her gaze to her wrist and frowned.

-I'm going home for supper.

-Can I come? I asked. I didn't even know I asked until I saw her hesitant sideways glare. I was quick to pull back, step away and put my hands up to signal no harm. Before I could walk away and condemn myself she looked at me and replied.

-Mama doesn't approve of boys, but maybe this once it'll be okay.

Those words reached me fast and I came close to her again and laughed. She laughed with me in a mimetic soft way. We walked together down the sidewalk, a healthy distance apart for another mile. We spilled through the nighttime grotto with the post dinner sitcoms flashing blue through windows.

Up against the harbor, on a backyard dock, a gull swept down to a greatest wrapper on the gravel drive. We reached her home. Snow gray hydrangeas guarded the front porch behind the expanse of lawn, a dripping verdure under my boots. Boots of my father that blistered the split pomegranate of my heel and made me wince when I walked uphill. Buttons told me to wait by the mailbox while she went inside to talk to Mama Buttons.

I turned my back to the house and picked my nose. Waiting and kicking a beetle from my shoelace, I started to think about the voices being raised, unseen to me like conspiring ghosts, deducing me to a horny manipulative adolescent. Standing in the rain and coughing, I felt ill and tired. The screen door swung open and rattled a neighboring flower pot in a tire. That smell of steam rising from wet asphalt and I smiled in brief recognition. Buttons stood behind her mother like a miniature replica, the same warm sorrel locks and sacrosanct stare.

-Come in, George. Mama Buttons commanded, holding the screen door and stitching my slumped gorilla posture with silent criticism. I hurried up the steps and into the house, a foyer with a bench and striped throw pillows, a brass bucket near the door mat crowded with umbrellas. The door was double locked and a ceiling light flipped on. Mama Buttons stood in front of me and put out a thin sallow right hand. The flaming red lacquered talons of her fingernails glinted in the light like fresh blood.

-Betty, she pronounced, assured and subtle like a realtor. In Betty's face I saw Buttons' dimpled chin and pale green eyes. I saw the same pink arch of a frown, and slightly beaked and freckled nose. Betty was no more than three years older than my sister, Doris, who married a silverware salesman in the southern county and had a little boy last year. Betty may have been younger than Doris for all I knew, it was eerie to see Betty by Buttons. Betty stood like the full culmination of feminine curvature, features clouded in cosmetic putties and earlobes dazzled with gems. Buttons bowed before Betty like the innocent fawn and fading mirage of Betty's youth.

I was led into a dining room with three plates circling a yellow ceramic pot with daisies sprouting out. The tablecloth was webby lace with spots of soup and dressing sponged up and crusted brown. A scratchy black pot was placed on a cotton rag and the lid removed, a thousand shivering wet eyes of steam clung to the surface. The stew was a pile of beef cubes and potato wedges, a side of peas and broccoli in cheese sauce.

Betty was drinking wine with dinner and poured a glass for Buttons and I to share. She spoke in rational lubricity, and inside myself I snickered at her vocabulary borrowed from those homely housewife book clubs. Her manners even made me chuckle, they were so precise and painfully rehearsed. As if she had waited a long time for a chance to perform them and revive interest in herself. Towards the end of dinner, I got sick, that illness I was repressing burst between my fingers and I sprinted to the kitchen sink because I didn't know where the bathroom was. I collapsed and the rest is nothing until I awoke much later.

Wrenching myself from the crevice of a couch, my head flew from its pillow and twitched in the darkness, confused and sweating. I got sick once more, heaving and choking on dinner. My body rolled off the couch onto the floor and I curled inside arms sheathed in pajamas of unknown origin. My shirt was caked with wax clumps of semi-digested starch. Buttons and Betty rushed into the room. Betty shrieked and Buttons retreated to a light switch by the door.

I found myself in the warm compromising bosom of Betty with my hair wet and stuck to my forehead and Betty's ripe wine breath. She cradled me tight, brave with mothering passion and bright flooding concern. As I closed my eyes into Betty's sheer loose nightgown I felt the light grasp of Button's fleshy mittens unraveling my drawstring pants and pulled them down to expose the light curling fuzz on my upper thighs.

My exhausted feverish limbs swung from Betty's embrace but she pinned my wrists, she wouldn't give me space and I started to get scared. Then I felt it, the warm clamp of Button's mouth and Betty kissed my lips to keep me quiet. Buttons lifted her face from me and Betty straddled me, removed a knife from a concealed pocket in her robe. She begged me to slash her breasts and stomach. I tried to worm away from her insistent gyrating hips. Buttons put the knife in my hand, curled her fingers around my grip and plunged at Betty's contracting abdomen. The garnet streams trickled to my chest and I sobbed as the foaming surge of grief and pleasure shot hot bolts on the carpet.

My triangle with the masochistic mother and subservient daughter continued despite the horror and fear of the first encounter. Something in me began to understand Betty's shameful urge to be sullied and hurting. I started to empathize with the deep forbidden pathology of self-loathing. I started to admire the healing flaky scabs. I started to relate the impetuous need to see all your pain and anger boil to the surface, to disclose physical evidence of its existence and prove that it wouldn't just stay in your head and torture you. I started to be soothed by the crepitating wonder in Betty's loud climax just as I slashed her. I felt like I was giving her the greatest satisfaction of any kind, soon abusing her was necessary for me to enjoy our activities too. Later on, Buttons began to ask for them. Build up her tolerance.

I was never home. Slept in my bed twice a week and my parents were shaken with curiosity and tender intrigue until they were so irritated and directionless that they left me alone. They told me they believed I was living an underground life, separate and illegal possibly from my daytime facade. I did not admit their correctness, nor did I admit my lifestyle. Instead I kept my secrets to myself and let them kill me slowly.

The eight day of spring I entered the Betty-Buttons household with a knife I purchased at the corner hardware store in Red Tunnel. It was a combat knife a vet from Korea sold off and the wood handle was warm and indented where his fingers clenched it. The tip of the blade was chipped and it was collecting dust in its rack on the wall. Got a good price for it, I even thought about naming it, but forgot to do so by the time I undressed and walked up the steps to the bedroom. Betty was sitting on the heater by an open window reading a book and I saw her as a child, just a flicker, a frame, of what she might have been like, and I was astonished.

-George! She shouted with a grinning cigarette in her face and a stripe of sweat narrowing her brow. Rushing into her arms, I let her tickle my neck with her nose until Buttons came in, yawning and sly. She was no longer the fragile menstruating teenage girl I met before our incestuous triad. Buttons became a defiled blockage of female adulthood. Her eyes were stained with pictures of erections and blood, atomic bombs and poverty, outrage and denial. A piece of me began to miss her, that I placed above lust and carnage before I entangled my loins in her household, the angel pseudo virginal Buttons.

Our mating dance progressed. I threw Betty down on the floor and Buttons tied her mother's wrists and locked the door, locked in the insanity and delight side by side like indistinguishable deformed twins. Mother and daughter, Betty and Buttons, were my wives of Red Tunnel, and I am damned.

I pulled out my knife I bought that day and boasted it to Betty as I twirled the naked shaft of metal under her nose. Bringing the knife down, I miscalculated the depth of the wound, man mad red tunnel. Betty was hurt and not the hurt we like, hurt in some hidden arterial path. The blood was spreading on the carpet, Buttons ran downstairs to the laundry room to retrieve towels. Betty was groaning and shifting her back on a blackened blouse she discarded from her unharmed torso moments before.

- We have to call an ambulance. Buttons told me as we stood above her mother, purpling. I didn't want to stay there and confront myself. How could I find the courage to explain my savage fetishism to the chief of police and my father's best friend? My clothes were arranged in a shambling fright as I tumbled down the steps and out the door, my bloody hands wiped on my pants before I hopped my bicycle and left the house. That house I learned and loved better than my own, with walls and halls and doors and windows that witnessed our sick fashions of love and laughter in speechless agreement.

I did not keep up on the trial, did not call home, and did not finish my education. Instead of finding an escape and clearing from the past, I was ambushed by the demons of thought. On an occasional sleepless morning, I might have pondered a penitentiary visit to Buttons. I was afraid to see her, afraid to see my town, afraid of my former self and any shred of ether I could salvage from the wreckage. Why are things end badly hated and scorned even though once, before the deception and crime, you were happy, really, truly, blindly happy? Why does the conclusion of our relationships define them?

These are questions larger than me or Betty or Buttons or Red Tunnel, and maybe I have no business meddling with notions of the heart. In the hostile reversion of memory and silly prolonging of parts of my life, I have found little truth. The only truth I am conscious to decide is that there is a part of every person beyond human touch and understanding. A place for no words of colors, speaks no trifling abodes and cliché verisimilitudes. It has no plaintive ideals, does not provide a moral, it only takes and represses. There is one special zenith of catharsis, and it is empty indifference, an uncharted and irretrievable blankness. Arrested in these moments of cheap ambivalence, I tell myself I don't care because it makes me think I can control how much I care. Then I can rest again.

Ugly

Penny Sidewalk had a big warm heart that loved every creature on the planet. Penny Sidewalk dreamt of flying through the sunset crimson caps of mountains, birds perched on her shoulders like Snow White. Penny Sidewalk was full of pain and she never got a break. Some say these things make you stronger, but Penny Sidewalk felt like aluminum foil crumpled by strangers when they stared at her. She was not pretty, she was not happy. There was no song and there was no wine, Penny Sidewalk was the girl with the lazy eye and scoliosis hunch, a damsel who resembled Lon Chaney on her good days. Penny Sidewalk we love you.

From preschool to grad school nobody befriended her. She was accustomed to leaning into the doorframes of universities and annotating the walls with her thoughts. Kicking dust down the bridge in early morning, walking nowhere. As a child, Penny Sidewalk remembered her mother placing a manicured hand on top of her onion-skin scalp, quietly rationalizing people can't comprehend great things. Little Brother avoided her in the schoolyard and wept behind a brick wall as his friends threw rocks at her. Procol Harem and Jefferson Airplane were Penny Sidewalk's friends, just like the rooster statue on the countertop and George the Turtle in his radioactive tank, getting a bath on Sunday.

"You're asking me to love you?" Billy Chrysanthemum repeated in shock in the junior high cafeteria, his friends snorting over their brown bagged bologna. "How could I love some freak like you?" He asked, rhetorical and reprimanding. Penny stood at the vending machine, shaking it and uttering machine gun noises. She would later face expulsion for bringing papa's shotgun to school, later facing multiple cures in the forms of Ph.D.'s and Prozac, evangelist keyboards and picnic beers, non-refundable schizophrenic sodas Peyote Steve offered, and later the empty cottage with a fondling aunt who loved her more than Billy Chrysanthemum.

Penny Sidewalk, dear old-darling with your wrinkled brow on a plastic mattress. Do not cast away the dollar bill under your doormat, do not cast away the bird shit in your hair because they chose you as their moving target. Penny Sidewalk, no one in the world deserves you. Penny, lovely freak of our melody, please don't touch Grandpa's blood pressure medication.

That soiled bra and scabbing blister on your chin are worthy. Your crooked mouth and sagging jaw belong in the arms of an apostle. Dawn waits for all the poison to seep away. Monday waits to be greeted with hung over scorn. Cousin Ben still has your sailboat you made with the children in the courtyard before they all ran away. Hollywood smiles will kiss your cheeks in dreams. The reservoir frozen over in March will feel like a shattered window when you fall through it, leading you back to a sky full of fish. Yes, your mother should have avoided Brandy in her second trimester, and yes, father is fucking the mailman, but it will be alright.

Autumn smells like sweat in the deli when you can't stand the daylight. The sun looks like a celestial cyst and the grass is reminiscent of the hairs you plucked from your arms that day Elise Vantello perspired in the locker room and digressed from her holiday hook up with John to Penny Sidewalk's body hair. Summer was better because you were alone, strumming your mandolin of self-pity as your fat wide flippers of feet sucked on the marble tiles of the bathroom floor as you prepared yourself for the afterlife. Forget winter, we all know how your snot likes to freeze like crystal lye on your nostrils, but remember spring for the Easter egg you filled with nails and fed to a cat behind Dominos.

It is said that at twenty you joined a convent but denounced the faith after you had a vision of copulating with Christ on the thorn bushes outside. It is said that you worked in a rubber lover factory but was fired after your boss discovered your tongue in the hole of a Nagasaki Venus in your blue pick-up during lunch hour. It is said that you've wandered all the way to Argentina to dangle scorpions over your ears and plead with God for a better harvest. It is said that somewhere an infant was placed in a tomb, and its single whimper was your name. It is said that you were born old and ugly, and that with infinity and fable they will unearth your corpse in a stellar pin up frame. It is said that your every marred pore was an unanswered prayer and that the tingly ferns below your pelvis shutter with butterflies. We believe these things, we do.

At forty-one and long past illusion, Penny Sidewalk discovered a bundle of bloody rags in the gutter. Penny scooped the mass from the moldy passages and cradled it in her arms, clutching the stained fabric to her breasts. Down the street and up the building into her flat, a door locked and a candle simmering in the dim terrarium of her room. Penny Sidewalk spun from the door to the couch, a cyclone spattered in blood, slow and empty, still on the floor with the monster sack of cloth. Penny Sidewalk unfolded the rags with a delicate fear, her plump pink fingertips gracing the cloth like the layers of a decomposing mandala.

A unicorn fetus, blacked in a clot of blood, glowing with a supernatural chaos in its swollen eyes, shifted on the carpet and Penny Sidewalk screamed. The horn in the center of its forehead was merely a flaccid gray stub and its hairless brown face writhed in a squeal, a nervous burst of discontent that fluttered through Penny's lip hair. Its snout ejected a faint rainbow and Penny Sidewalk felt a sudden bowel movement seize her. Penny Sidewalk was uncertain of why she had taken the bundle from the gutter, wrapped in fairy tale placenta and gauze, looking like a rejected Sunday meat or a hog's head in bandages. The unicorn fetus whispered an oath of obscurity in the gutter, nothing was so daring in its audacity to defy reality and she adored this outcast, this alien, discarded and disassociated from society like her. She would be its mother and raise it.

But what if this unicorn died on the floor, where could she bury it and could she resist the temptation to unearth its cadaver from the soil and taste the clay mud of the grave for further fantasy? If it grew and remained in the flat, could it gallop from the kitchen to the bedroom happily? Did it take one parent or two to maintain its mystical hygiene? Would it listen to Brahms and eat the algebra textbook before she surrendered her notions of motherhood? Could she give this unicorn fetus the wonderful childhood she never had, and would it leave her one day, ungrateful and immortal in its supremacy to science? Could this orphaned Pegasus dream? There was only one way to know.

Penny Sidewalk debated calling her older sister, Margaret in Maine about this. But Margaret was busy, balancing a toddler on her left hip and crushing the phone buttons on her shoulder as she stirred tomato sauce on a gas stove. Margaret would tell Penny Sidewalk the same advice she offered since they were children. To see help from the psychiatric salvation on fifth and north. But what did Margaret know of magic in the inebriated clutches of her husband? Nobody had tasted such loneliness and nobody resurrected a longing in Penny Sidewalk she had long thought died out with Billy Chrysanthemum and the rest of the hippies.

After sitting in the lily pad bean-bag chair in the corner for twenty minutes, Penny approached the unicorn once more.

"If we're going to live together I have to give you a name." she mused while lowering her wrist to its forehead, squinting at its tiny hooves that resembled coals. After staring at the silver atoms on the static television she named the fetus Opal because of the graying pale orb of its stomach that rose with every wheezing yawn. She stroked its neck and briefly stifled a sob of joy and admiration. Eight days later, Opal was dead in the crib Penny Sidewalk fashioned from chair legs and throw pillows. She awoke at ten am, heading to the kitchen for baby formula and apple sauce, only to reach the crib and poke Opal's spine with her index finger until she released a scream that unglued the wallpaper. Penny had just started to get used to having Opal around, it wasn't weird anymore and she was no longer afraid it was a hallucination. This unicorn fetus, left in the gutter waiting for her, had crossed over a boundary of comprehension

and disappeared as quickly as it came. After Opal died, Penny Sidewalk had difficulty returning to her life with the same enthusiasm. She lived every day with a waning tolerance, subject to pangs of remorse. *I could have checked in on him at midnight instead of waiting till morning. I could have built a better crib. I could have taken its picture and stolen glimpses of it at my desk as the hands of the clock spun in a prosaic tedium.*

Back to the world, you've had your fund. Back to the grind of living and dying with all those people you never had time to fully know. Back for more, waking each day with a suppressed hope for someone to nurture you. We say these things with love in our hearts, Penny Sidewalk, remember the climb and remember the fall, we were always there.

Crooked Fish Tots

We were still little. Little enough that I thought I was the shit and you followed along. I was the one standing as you sat down, in our backyard inflatable pool Cindy filled with the garden hose. I hated that pool. Sticks and leaves floated on the surface and you Millis, my friend until the end, wiggled your pearly fat toes under the water. Telling me about the flaky metallic green nail polish you saw your mom swipe from the pharmacy. She painted your fingernails to keep you from telling Daddy.

Cindy, our babysitter, was inside the house. Reading a magazine, rifling through our possession. Smoking. Every time I crawl back into my dim fragmented nine-year-old thoughts of that summer, Cindy is frowning at me. That cigarette, the white pillar with a crow of ash between her knuckles, glares at me in its stringy smoke curling under those safety pinned earlobes. I grew up with Cindy, my mother's friend's daughter. Cindy wore combat boots with ripped plaid laces, fishnet stockings and chained and pleated skirts. All articles of clothing frayed and torn like she set her cat on fire and the cat won. Eyes. Acid yellow slits shifting under her furry shelf of mascara. One year Cindy came to Thanksgiving with a shaved head. Everyone called her Luke. For Leukemia.

In our town of Crooked Fish, everyone lived and died under the supervision of the god-fearing commissioner. Bursts of gossip were incarnate in a divorce or a suspect community of migrant workers. Crooked Fish was one of the many receptacles of freshly married yuppies, soon to be breeding. An affluent bedpan to shed all your nerve conditions and extramarital curiosities in beautiful smiling lawn gnome secrecy. The wealthiest married the wealthiest to maintain their human horticulture; condescending to the working-class town of Shickinny Pass nearby. Such natural inequalities were soothing in the face of growing communal hysteria. Pastel porch chairs. Punctual systematic sprinklers. Mailboxes painted with birds; erect at a perfect angle from the ground. Newspapers placed at the end of every driveway. A population pouched in the wester crags of the county.

My mom was a single mother and excluded from most of Crooked Fish. The only person to enter our house without soliciting or repairing anything was Cindy's mother, a fellow outcast with a daughter that neighbors called a gothic witch to behead. My babysitter. The only job in town that didn't discriminate against her sulky surreal anti-social guise. When I grew up I became something very similar to Cindy. A monster.

Todd was Cindy's boyfriend her mother hated. Cindy could only see Todd when she was at my house, babysitting Millis and I, when neither my mother nor her mother could object. To buy our silence, Todd bought us each a Barbie from the dollar mart. I was insulted, I was too old at the time to accept Barbies in public. My doll was blonde just like me. Millis' doll was a brunette just like her. This won special favor from both of us. Children implicated in the strange inner lives of adults was natural in Crooked Fish.

In July it was so hot that Millis threw up on the swing set. Cindy agreed to fill up the inflatable pool only if I blew it up. I let Millis borrow my bathing suit even though she was a fat little thing. I let her stretch out my least favorite two-piece. In return, Millis let me bully her about a purple scar from a barbecuing accident on her forehead.

After Cindy gave us hotdogs she asked if Todd could take a picture of Millis and me for a high school photography class assignment. Cindy even put some of her chunky black eyeliner on me and gave me one earring to wear. I thought I looked like Debbie Harry. Todd's baggy stained clothes on his skinny pale figure made me think of the homeless veteran outside our grocery store. As he took out his camera, Millis didn't bother standing up, she knew she was the ugly one and I deserved the spotlight.

Striking a stare and crossing my arms, I tried to be like the ladies in the magazines Cindy read in the house. Magazines plastered with insecure questions about menstruation or hair spray. As I stood in my momentary fame, Cindy leaned forward and handed me her cigarette. Smoke it! The shutter of the camera clapped hungrily upon me and every thread of smoke that got in my eyes produced a tiny tear I did not blink away.

Todd's elbows pulled into his sides and the camera hung against his small chest. He heaved in satisfaction, like he was observing a landmark. Take off your suit. He said. Cindy nodded to me. And I did. I waited. Armored in my anger as Millis matched my fear behind me. Todd did not take my picture. He fished my bathing suit out of the inflatable pool and squeezed himself into it. The waistband of my bottoms pinched his white skin, glistening from the water that just clung to me. He handed me the camera, asking for his picture. I took it. And I never took it away.

What are you doing? Mom called from the patio.

VanAuston's Wildest Dreams

VanAuston combed crisp with his tie a narrow navy flap between pectorals tanned and the model of physical excellence. His anagrammed, ironed, bleached, starched, and collared white shirt with black shell buttons descending down his six pack to a crocodile leather belt holding up khakis. Shoes imported Italian and golden cufflinks with a Princeton class ring tight around his hairless pinky. Signature beige handkerchief folded in his breast pocket and a seven-diamond Rolex on his left wrist, a Christmas present from his contractor in Nicaragua.

Hair slicked to the scalp in a perfumed gel, wavy flaxen locks smoothed back from his face. His face had pores immaculate and empty of greasy bourgeois. Exfoliated to perfection, clean and flawless with the efforts of a dermatologist with prices that formed wrinkles. VanAuston was sculpted and groomed like a sun god, a shaven Plutocrat with a revival for splendor.

Bachelor of twenty-nine. Brilliant magnate with multiple biographers chronicling his prodigal climb to becoming the wealthiest man in the country. Hypnotic and notorious womanizer with an embracing, bottomless charisma. He was a corporate supervisor of a skyscraper construction company in Los Angeles. His methodical ascension from managerial apparatus to full-time administrator brought the iciest jewels and costumes of luxury. Twenty-nine and the paragon of opulence, an unreal image of polished aristocracy. A scalding business tycoon, the simulacrum of the glorious pampering whose decadence made him a heretic.

Evenings he frequents five-star restaurants with various girlfriends of his department's interns. He met these women at the company's holiday party and seduced each now. He is now at eight. Each girl asked VanAuston to keep their date a secret, leaning over their calligraphed menus and their lip gloss shimmering in the candlelight. *Please don't tell my boyfriend, I've just never been on a date with a billionaire before.*

Parade the girls with the best wines, finest bouquets, limo rides to a high-rise condo with floor to ceiling windows overlooking the entire city. Throw the cheapest trinkets their way and they're unbuckling him in the elevator. There is a VanAuston Children's Hospital, a VanAuston Country Club, a VanAuston Construction Company, a VanAuston Charity Foundation. He has an Astin Martin that can reach 220 miles per hour in thirteen seconds. Mansions in Beverly Hills, Rio de Janeiro, Paris, and Venus. Condos in Los Angeles, Palm Beach, and New York City. Dinner guest of Nelson Mandela, Mark Zuckerberg, and Hugh Hefner. Periodic one-night stand of supermodel, heiress, monarch, movie star. He has a pilot's license and flies jets when he's not golfing with Bill Gates.

When the days get long and the charts look unsteady, when statistics worm their way into his dreams and multiply in numbers of calculating torment, VanAuston hops a plane to the farthest exotic location. Safari bungalows and luncheons across from prostitutes with the cleverest sneers at his approaches. He found himself to poor hookers because they didn't want to stay around. The other women posed themselves by VanAuston as possible marital endeavors and called back in the morning. Grit and poverty with hostels of sensual yet impressionable refugees begging for a meal was his infatuation. Smoldering in his arms, they were his only tangible relation to horror left in his prosperity that disenchanted him. The only remains of filth and squalor he scrubbed off his manicured hands. One more vehicle of the Global North dominating the Global South. He loved it when they would undress in skeptic precision, gripping him in feverish captivity. They dissolved his grim aphotic affluence and ensnared his snobbish demeanor with carnal impulse.

There was something irreplaceable about a Moroccan bazaar with thirteen-year-old girls standing by meat carts. Something irreplaceable about Sudanese orphanages with nymphs chained to kitchen heaters. Something irreplaceable about Kiev brothels at dawn. Something irreplaceable about swimming and coalescing with the bosom of a frowning pubescent methamphetamine motivated single mother of two.

Obscured in Cimmerian void of a basement bar with posture stiff and magnificent while lulling a child from their pimp, bewitched by a subversive gremlin in a miniskirt. This is the key to VanAuston's shriveled black heart: the tang of a tramp in an alley. Grenade to his heart, won by agents of chaos. Softened in the resentful pout of a concubine, no other pleas for comfort will sound.

Coming home from the trips was the difficult part. Returning to marvel foyer, oil paintings, tanning bed and valium medicine cabinet was difficult. Getting back into the function of his dysfunction, manifested in alcoholism, satyriasis, materialism and Machiavellian integrity to smile for clients. To shake hands and promise the best promise language can fabricate. Being interviewed by *Forbes, Newsweek*, and *Esquire*. Being hounded by media microphones about how his expenses lubricate his folly. Hiding out on a yacht off the coast of Majorca, sleeping on silk bed sheets and waking up in febrile paranoia. Atlas under thirty.

His family bothered him for money often until last month when his Father broke into his condo and tried to kill him. Since then, VanAuston established a restraining order from every immediate relative and avoided contact with strict, callous indifference. His roots have grown into him and won't let him breathe. He's just a bank account to them. A name they can attach themselves to in an attempt to fortify their own pathetic aspirations. A blood connection they can claim ownership to, a family bond with a first of steel strapped in capitalist dynamite.

Friendships are solidified in acquisitions and there is not a deed he can divulge in confidence without bouncing back in the voice of a stranger. His housekeepers are fired regularly for stealing. Fellow entrepreneurs encouraged VanAuston to enter politics and splurge on a lavish campaign and settle behind a podium. He's a prime candidate: vibrant, young ivy-league spawn and an exclusively enticing genius orator. They said he could win any office he wanted and that's why he won't run at all.

Corporate collusions were his best trade. He knew all the best locations, best stocks, when to invest, when to withdraw, when to arrive, when to decide. It was an intuitive talent, something like Picasso or

Mozart, just some natural intrinsic understanding. His fortune in currency, handsomeness, intellect, and savvy innovative audacity cemented his path to his goals. A religion of Fort Knox pharaohs in a patriotic landslide, a doctrine in prolific monolithic intensity. Panoptic economic comprehension, it was a gift he could not articulate under the gaze of envious reporters. On numerous occasions he's been compared to Carnegie, Rockefeller, Getty, Morgan. Financial advisors sift through his bowel movements for sapphires, his opinion the guidance of God.

A year ago, women started emerging and claimed to have VanAuston's children. He paid off every skank and shield his bloodshot blue eyes under Armani sunglasses, dodging paparazzi in plazas and spitting on cyclists that rammed his security guards on the sidewalk. Half the public is enamored with his kingly prowess while the other half, stunned in the recession, unemployed and protesting, demonizes him on internet forums and calls him the embodiment of consumerist disease.

As a birthday gift to himself, Van Auston purchased a building with six floors, thirty-four apartments and an indoor pool. He had bars installed in the windows and all the doors lockable only from outside hallways. Rooms furnished with a fridge of fruit and dairy, a television, and a dishwasher. No telephones, no balconies, no computers, an intercom and a staff of former SWAT members that offer no form of connection to the outside world. They were directed by VanAuston simple and clear: nobody leaves the building alive.

Over the course of three weeks, VanAuston returned to all his previous getaways and kidnapped prostitutes that once replaced his dread with orgasms. He lured them on planes and dangled sparkling adventures in their gaunt faces. They couldn't get enough of it. Once on the place they were heavily sedated and taken to a private location with a trailer that drove fifty three miles to the detainment building where they would be housed for the rest of their lives.

VanAuston bought, gutted, redesigned a warehouse twenty miles from his detainment building. The warehouse was a towering cement island in a fenced off lot, the nearest resident six miles away. The warehouse has a reproduction facility. There are eight mattresses on the floor with chains attached to the floor beside it.

Detainment building has a basement with a boxing ring where the women will fight each other to the death. With the warehouse reproduction facility and the detainment building working together, Van Auston will have a dynasty of sex slaves whom he is teaching to hate their own gender by killing each other. They will be afforded few tools to aid in their slaughter. One gets a bat. One gets an axe.

This idea sprung from VanAuston's loneliness. It was loneliness not from a greed of material or sexual hunger but of pure blind driven anxiety to have reigning command over whatever he wanted. These girls have been hardened by their lives yet society is desensitized to their suffering, they're already dead.

The weekends, VanAuston stopped dating the department interns' girlfriends and devoted his time to his slaves despite no material profit. Currently there are thirty girls abducted. Ten are pregnant and therefore not forced into the ring. Van Auston had to discipline them last week because he found a half-eaten girl under the staircase. You may ask: why would a man with the world at his feet do such a thing? Simple. Because he could.

There was a truly awkward moment last Thursday. VanAuston went to a board of trustees meeting on the thirty seventh floor and there was a blood stain on his thigh. From one of those girls. He cancelled the meeting right away, burned the pants, called and berated his dry cleaner. Broke down lachrymose and sobbing, shrieking with nostril goo dripping on his desk. Van Auston shedding tears of actual humiliation.

Memorial Day weekend, Van Auston fled the office early to perform new fatherly duties in the detainment building. His first child was going to be born today. He's buttoned his shirt wrong. Jogged to the limo in front of the building, giggling and slapping his chauffeur on the back as he opened the door.

"It's gonna be a boy. I got a great feeling"

"What are you talking about? Are we going to the hospital?"

"No"

"Are you alright, sir?"

"Of course, I am, don't I look alright? I have no idea what the hell you're talking about."

"Yes, sir"

Car ride, VanAuston shuffled papers in his briefcase to ease himself. Casually stroked his left eyebrow and chewed his lip.

"That's it, I'll call you later" Van Auston yelled over his shoulder, sauntering past the fence.

"Goodnight, sir"

VanAuston sprinted to the elevator and headed to room 5B. Stretching, deep breathing. Lunged into 5B with his arms open, grinning. A toothpaste green smock was thrown on him and he hurried into the bedroom. A girl of sixteen was screaming.

He missed it. The child was already born, squirming like a purple goblin. It looked like a worm, or a radish, or some terrible blob with piercing squeals.

"Let me see my child!" VanAuston declared, elbowing toward the pink bundle, removing the cloth.

"It's a girl!" VanAuston wailed, throwing the baby down and jumping on it. He threw his smock on the chair and slammed the door behind him.

The Best Kind of Friends

Without deception the truth would have no value. Without deception there would be no happiness. Deception breathes every day in every trembling sign on every lip somewhere, somehow, we deceive even when we don't mean to. We deceive ourselves, and we're only conscious of a fraction of it. Deception makes money and fills sleeves with bills from criminals and taxpayers. It wears clothing, tastes, laughs, and farts. Deception is the oldest friend and surviving basic instinct in civilization. Make friends with deception, practice the code and you can slither through the cracks indefinitely.

Shovel split soil on Rocky Pandora, a town forty miles west of the Michigan border. Foot first, Iguana Arkansas spit the snus he bought three hours ago into the pit he'd dug with Forever Skins, his partner and colleague. Forever Skins was a man with smoky white hair that fell frayed and dry to his shoulders, center part like a Puritan. He liked to wear a blue carnation in his lapel, earning the name, *blue gut*, because when he dug graves the petals would scatter along his shirt in cerulean buds.

Partner and pal, Iguana Arkansas was a West Point dropout who engrossed himself late into the night with periodicals on the Afghan War, clipping passages that went into a swollen black macassar ebony desk, never read once more. His cheeks were puffy perpetual pink from shaving constantly, nails cut close to the quick for no dirt to gather while digging. A small pointed burn on from an iron was above the abdomen of his shirt and the trousers were pin striped, clean narrow lines down his thighs.

"Smells like shit down here" Iguana muttered with his undershirt over his nose.

"Man can get used to anything" Forever replied, unphased by the enveloping miasma, sticking to their foreheads and sinking in their pores. Like a machine, the repetition of down in ground-out over shoulder was natural to Forever. A function like urinating or chewing, never stopping to stammer.

Eight years ago, Forever's wife, Dolores, died of kidney failure and he swore he's been abstinent since. Iguana scoffed at hearing this, crossing his arms and shaking his head in pity. *You're young, you don't understand love*, Forever asserted aloud to Iguana one evening. Insulted but unresponsive out of respect for the humble widower, Iguana avoided the subject and the men formed a reliance on each other. Boss loved Iguana like his favorite son. Forever Skins told Boss from the beginning that Iguana Arkansas wasn't cut for the work and that he was better off as a notary somewhere, some money hungry dog catcher. After a couple heists and homicides, Forever admitted an unexpected fondness of Iguana because he made him melancholy for his tenacious brother that died in college.

"I wonder what poor soul would miss this bastard" Iguana asked while gazing at rapidly mounting dirt, leaning on a shovel and stalling.

"The hell you care. Man's a dead man" Mud on his jaw and eyes on a finger poking through the first, Forever sighed, "Wanna get some food after this?"

Andy's Fork and Knife was a diner off the interstate five mails from the Candid Inn where Iguana Arkansas and Forever Skins would spend the night after a meal that couched the intestines comfortably and satiated Forever's frugality. Secluded in a corner booth with squeaky vermillion cushions, the smell of burnt wedges of toast was a relief. Iguana loosened his yellow argyle tie as Forever rolled a cigarette on the laminated menu. It was that time of day where the sun bled through cornfields like a broken vessel in golden tundra.

"You got kids, Forever?"

"I do and they don't want nuthin' with me"

"Don't blame 'em" A muffled laugh escaped Iguana in the napkin he smoothed across his stubbled chin. Forever pinched some curly brown strands of tobacco on the table and threw them at Iguana. Coffee came in chipped enamel and spilled in the saucers beneath them, the waitress smiled and Iguana found her thin upper lip attractive.

"What's the special today?" Iguana asked eager with his hands in his lap and toes curled in his shoes.

"The peach co…"

"She's special enough Arkansas, what you worried about?" Forever interrupted, chuckling while tucking his napkin in his collar and winking at Iguana.

"The peach cobbler and key-lime" The waitress finished, pressing a spiral notepad to her chest. Her name tag read Lila.

"We'll have two of those. Thank you very much, Lila" Iguana resounded, stretching a grin. Forever raised his eyebrow and his smirk behind the menu. Ivory neck supple and violet glitter nail polish scratching her left arm, Lila turned and left with the retreating pink cotton bow of her apron under lusty surveillance.

"You should totally fuck her" Forever mused, stirring three creams and a sweet n low in his coffee.

Iguana slapped his hands on the table and slid forward beaming.

"You think so?"

"She's prime for pickin', fool" Forever answered, sipping his coffee. Iguana picked up a toothpick from the tray near the window and jabbed at his gums until Lila came back with two plates.

"There ya go. Two cobblers and key-limes" Lila spoke, crisp and projecting a dim smile, wiping her sweaty pale hands on her smock and studying her sneakers.

"When you get off work, Li-lah?" Iguana plunged, sticking a fork straight up in his cobbler and letting it slowly fall over. She seemed surprised by Iguana and tightened her lips and looked at Forever.

"Not until 10:30, sorry"

Utter disappointment that failed concealment burbled under Iguana's face muscles.

"That's alright, another time the. I'll be back-fer-ya" Iguana reassured her, pronouncing the last syllables hastily and tense. The sound of utensils hitting porcelain and a sizzling pan became more apparent. Lila nodded and smiled back, curling her hands into fists before sailing back into the kitchen.

"You're hilarious" Forever laughed with gelatinous green goo dribbling onto his lip.

A heavy rust colored coach bag weighted with 80k from Boss sat in Iguana's lap as Forever drove to the Candid Inn. The Lila incident ceased mentioned after Iguana punched Forever in the gravel parking lot behind their neon blue mustang. Sore in the shoulders and aching in the elbows, Forever steered the vehicle in subtle resentment with car radio blaring. Bitter from being coaxed into a trap, Iguana spat snus out the window and the wind blew it back on the side of the mustang, to which Iguana watched the glob roll down the door in the rearview mirror.

This dusty two-story island stood before a wooden signed caved jagged CANDID INN, the first three letters faint. Swatting his tongue on the roof of his mouth, Iguana sucked the brown fluid through the cracks in his teeth before entering the building. Adjusting his sterling cufflinks before tapping the bell despite the pock marked cronie frowning in a swivel chair a yard away. Forever shoved road map pamphlets on the counter aside to lean forward and prop his elbows on spilt soda.

"Two rooms" Forever declared.

The coach bag was held in Iguana's hand from a stringy right arm. He followed Forever and the cronie down the hall and a segway past a pool with an inflatable shark bobbing lonely near a vent. Resting a hand on the railing as the chronie unlocked the separate rooms, Iguana watched Forever tuck a bill in the cronie's breast pocket and Iguana felt a private urge to attack him. Forever noticed Iguana's disdain.

"Relax. Extract that metal rod from your ass" Forever shrugged before slamming his door. Tightening his grasp on the coach bag, Iguana grit his teeth and reached for his snus in his pocket before walking into his room.

Midnight vodka bath didn't calm Iguana. Stumbling across the carpet, reciting insults in his head like futile ammunition. The sickness might creep through his cavity after two more hours, but he was too busy fuming in the peach painted walls. Feeling isolated, kicking himself from one grave to another, mustang-Forever Skins' style. Rubbing the invincible needle scars on his arm, thrown between cynical alienated auditorium to self-loathing closet. Forever was right. He was too manic and orderly for this crop of creation.

By one he was more drunk than he wanted to be. Spread on the bed with his hands over his face, he put on his suit and went outside for air. Reloading his mouth with snus, obscene laughter aborted the gap of silence between the door and railing. Turning an angry eye on the doors behind him, he sat on the rail and cupped an ear to identify the direction of the cackling. Some insane sonata ricocheted off the concrete walls and it tingled under Forever Skins' door.

But like the best things, we never seem to think they're actually happening. Inching towards the door with feet dragging, Iguana nudged open Forever's door. *Unlocked, dumb shit.* All fours with mammaries swinging, dear Lila. Iguana pulled the door back to him, leaving a spare crack to watch. He listens to the slapping of skin and his partner's simian grunts. One of Forever's crumpled blue carnations was ground into the carpet.

Door shut. Step away. Let it go. Handling himself pretty well for an angry drunk, Iguana returned to his room and threw scattered shirts back into his suitcase. Items once meticulously matched in a fantastic disarray of pastel and gray. Whimsical click and coach bag tucked between arm and rib, he locked the door and headed to the parking lot. Boss will come after him and maybe Forever might bury him. Maybe even perform a cruel and unusual autopsy to set an example. Deception, friends, lurking in your origins and embedded in your eyes, can't win.

Alligator Spitfuck and the Purple Dip-Shits

They said I'd never make anything of my life. That I'd be fat and broke like my parents, crazy burn out bum with no prospects. Faced many confrontations in the form of disciplinarians, politicians, organizations, populations. My career is explosive in this battlefield against the public's conception of what's wrong. I have a monopoly on the future rock star generation. Yes, there was darkness, violence on the self and others. But you always need a little blood for the sharks to smell.

My name is Alligator Spitfuck. Got it on the stage of the Tequila Take Down in L.A. with my band the Purple Dip-Shits. Leader singer: myself, bassist: Hooker Cash, guitarist: Daytime Suicide, and drums: Butthole AIDS.

Hooker Cash and Daytime Suicide wanted to break up the band last year after Daytime had an affair with Hooker's wife. Hooker went into Daytime's dressing room while we were shooting the music video "Serial Killer Christ" and kicked the mirrors. Ashtrays turned over on the candy-red carpet and the couch musty of urine. Butthole AIDS was drunk somewhere outside, smoking and talking up an assistant.

Rolling Stone was our latest tabloid bid, got some raving reactions about gluing my naked body with bloody money. Lot of followers on my twitter asked me if it hurt to peel off the bills afterwards. Answer: no, I kissed every Benjamin. Oprah boycotted my music because she said it was degrading to women. I'm thrilled, periodicals put my name with these little asterisks and that makes me laugh. Who do they think they're fooling? The asterisks only bring me more attention.

I was on a plane from London to New York and Jeremy Irons sat next to me. I was expecting him to have an Italian silk vest, a monocle and Cuban cigar. Instead he looked like my agent, crisp black suit with an ascot labeled: *suave motherfucker*. Stewardess swung by with a tray of bottles. When I awoke in my hotel eight hours later hung over, I was mortified that I told Jeremy Irons my secret fantasy. One day I wanted to make enough money to pay him to speak for me. I could float in my pool and nod at Jeremy on the diving board who would harshly direct to my servant: *Alligator needs more whiskey.*

The coke party after the Grammy's was at Courtney Love's house. I think she's a piece of shit but I love her daughter. I can't come back because last time I got wasted I ended up chasing her neighbor's pets across the lawns naked. You think she'd be okay with that sort of thing.

When I die I want them to put the titles of all my songs on my headstone. I want to be cremated, my ashes ingested by my ex-wives.

Heroine, why did you love me so much? Rehab one. Rehab two. Rehab three. Okay I'm a music god cliché. There's something wrong with this society that inhibits me from living my life to its fullest. I've reached a point now where I'm just a face on a T shirt, a symbol for the revolution. Sometimes I get asked how long I plan to be a rock star, like being a baseball player or a model, having to admit that my age could stunt my career. In our business it's the men that tear themselves down. How could you not? Everywhere I look something tells me what I don't have.

Betty White likes her silver cotton candy sprinkled. I hope the next Pope is black. The best porn will come out after that.

Butthole AIDS can't make it to the concert tonight. His lawyer called about statutory rape. Reporters are gonna piss all over me with questions, expecting me to speak on his behalf. Hooker Cash and Daytime Suicide will blame me because I saw Butthole pull that groupie into the trailer. My entire life I never asked myself if I went too far. Rock rebellion and resurrection, I've been searching for a boundary I can't break, an eccentric irony. I'm so easy to convict.

As I do in all times of fear and distress, I call my best friend. David Bowie. Straight to voicemail. I called himself last year when I was robbed by a Vietnamese hostess.

The cops will probably be here by noon, I have to bury the pills outside. I smoked a cigarette in the kitchen, Ziploc candy and a spade in my left hand. Before I left I put on my dad's wool hunting hat he gave me when I was a teenager. It looked like a llama hide on your head. He called it his hat of knowledge and wore it as a joke. He greeted my prom date on the lawn wearing it. Since he's been dead I've worn it a lot.

Went into the woods behind the mansion, past the pool and down the path leading to a creek. Fifteen feet on the left side of the creak, near the willow, I buried my stash. Once the ground was reaffirmed, I rubbed the fine black mud between my fingers under the creek's brackish water. Threw water on my neck and across my face, my breath smelled like shit and beer.

I was taking the path I always take back from the creek. The house was in sight. Glinting rectangles of my windows fanned by leaves. Pine cones crunched under my jack boots. The sunlight hadn't gained the color of afternoon. It was still glaucoma gray in morning. A freefall in a four by four dug in the path and covered with leaves. There have been many times in my life, whether it was hurrying from a bistro to a limo or being grated in a beige armchair across from my ex-wife and her lawyer, that I just wanted to the ground to open up and swallow me.

On my back, looking up through the ring of dirt above me cradling an egg shell sky. Tried to lift my arms but couldn't. Tried to lift my legs but couldn't. There were sharpened sticks in the bottom of this pit, covered with feces. I could smell it in the blood on my clothes. Jagged points of bark black and foul with shit. I looked like a mannequin on a bed of thorns. If I get out alive I want my wheelchair gold plated.

Mustering a scream, I opened my mouth and coughed blood. None of this is happening. That's what they always say. Thumbs twitching, lips cracked white trembling. Crumbs of soil in my eyes, catching the shades of two friends above.

"Spitfuck." They repeated. Voice came together in the most delectable union. Familiar folks these vocal chords pronounced in me. Turned my head to the left and clenched my bloody teeth from the stick driving into my jaw. Grunting, I reassured myself I could. Hooker and Daytime Suicide stood above me passing a flask.

"We heard. We know what you did with our money" Daytime Suicide ejected the words in a jet of smoke. His arms crossed over the leather jacket with a lime green swastika on the lapel.

"We found that Vietnamese hostess from last year. She's HIV positive. We figured this would be a better way to die for you" Hooker Cash laughed, placing hands on his head and grinning a sigh, "Butthole AIDS is gonna go to prison and the Purple Dip-Shits belong in the past. Everybody was right. What we created was immortal and too great to last"

Hooker stopped talking and turned his profile to the shutters shaking against the house in the wind. Daytime threw a lit cigarette in the pit and it burned through my pants. Worms and spiders are my playmates. My carcass is my playmate. My death is my playmate. Born and died in the name of shit.

Daytime picked up two shovels and tossed one to Hooker because he wasn't worth the reach. Both began to bury me alive for the next three hours.

I suffocated. Piles of dirt thrown into my vortex before I crumble under the onslaught. My mouth filled with the ash of my tomb. Shovels broke sky and rained black. Choking on dirt, I did not sob. Did not beg. Did not plead for explanation. Took it like a martyr. Took it like a saint. Took it like a god.

My soul left my body. I hung over the ground and headed back to the mansion where I sat on the balcony smoking. Prepared some vinyl Velvet Underground until the cops came. Standing in the peeling gray sunlight on the wall paper of my kitchen, arms crossed and shaking my head. *Nope, cold, colder, Good, warm, warmer.* I told the police as they searched the house for my shotgun. They can't hear me and I wish I couldn't hear them. When I saw all my brothers in blue storming the house, I laughed giddy shouting: *I didn't know pigs traveled in packs!*

According to CNN, MSNBC, ABC, I'm missing. You're all saying I'm on the run from authorities and people have claimed to have spotted me in my hometown. Daytime Suicide and Hooker Cash are ducking paparazzi and declining comment. My agent is standing behind a podium with twelve microphones snaked under his chin. Camera bulbs flashed in his eyes that are otherwise soulless.

My lovely German shepherd, Hiroshima, found me. Man's best friend, the maid followed him down the path. Hiroshima dug two feet and we knew this was no ordinary game. The feces in my wounds were traced back to Daytime Suicide and Hooker Cash. The Purple Dip-Shits are legend.

Eulogy. Lines around the block. Police taped off the streets because sports cars blocked traffic. Felt badly for my children, the ex-wives pulled them in separate directions and shielded their eyes from flashbulbs.

The Elysian fields are opened once every millennium but if I feel like wreaking havoc on earth I am always free to do so. I'm looking for John Wayne Gacy to show me his handcuff trick.

I watched Butthole AIDS decompose in a cell, curled fetal position on his cot. I watched Daytime Suicide place his hand on Plexiglas to his wife and mouth sentimental chaos. I watch Hooker Cash hang himself with bedsheets, dangling from a ceiling pipe, ankles kiss by dust. Type our names in. You'll find a flaming dumpster of articles on every scrap of our existence riddled with media bias. Infinite books, memorabilia, tribute tours, parodies, peddler interviews. Alligator Spitfuck & the Purple Dip-Shits: the limited edition in pristine condition. Radio may bounce my bars through the waves, some teenager will wear my face, and some album will be pirated. We were a band that defied the ages by falling to it.

I could be mad. We all had some vulture circling our crowns. Abandon your expectations, this life will bury them.

Bastard in Chains

The office of psychiatrist Wyndam Gray was as cold and quaintly arranged as he was. Two hardwood chairs were placed on opposite sides of a door tacked with leaflets of blue skies and boxy yellow cottages his children's' imaginations had manifested on copy paper. There was the minute square of a window veiled in cobwebs above a bookcase containing volumes on Aristotle and illuminations that only graced Wyndam Gray with their presence in the thick archaic boldness of their fonts under the haze of a green desk lamp. It smelled like a bank. The walls emitted a stench of fresh paint and the stack of envelopes on his desk was placed by a framed portrait of his wife.

Dolly, his wife, the wafer slim silhouette of his childhood romps had evolved into an elegant brunette with social stature and assuring winks through a curtain. She would not speak to Wyndam. He was still living in the house but the past week he slept on the black leather sofa in the adjacent room with the coffee maker and water tank, turning his face into a mesh hand woven throw pillow that felt like a kidney stone in the temple when the night didn't end quick enough.

Dolly worked at the courthouse on the other side of town and threatened to change the locks when she had an argument with Wyndam on the patio. Sunday, her evenly tanned hands clenched the lapels of her fuzzy periwinkle bathrobe, grinding a pink house slipper into the pavement as her posture stiffened.

Wyndam loved Dolly and it wasn't her fault what he did. He knew it looked bad, she was embarrassed and embittered by his infidelity with a patient and mentioned it callously while glaring at the running faucet of the bathroom sink, standing in front of the fogged oval of the mirror as she combed her wet black hair that plastered down her back like paint. Wyndam wanted to embrace her, but she projected dim melancholy and reproachful sighs when he placed his hand on her shoulder at their son's soccer game. Dolly told the children about their father and this was a constant source of irritation for Wyndam. His son and daughter in grade school began talking to their Labrador, Houdini, about situations where the sun and moon don't like each other and won't be together but they'll still see both separately.

Wyndam's nineteen-year-old son, Robbie, from a previous marriage, retreated into the black light poster cave of his room, psychedelic mushroom painting placed above the laundry basket with cotton socks welded together with semen sprung from the VHS tapes under the floorboards. Robbie asked Wyndam who the woman was and what she did for a living, and Wyndam was slightly disconcerted by his son's curiosity. Wyndam recited her name and occupation once more, recalling the month of their affair's arrival and abruptly accompanying these descriptions with a vow of abstinence and shame.

Recently though Robbie did not leave the house and did not leave himself or those pubescent catastrophes and erratic hormones Wyndam chuckled at recalling his own. At dinner the other night, Dolly confirmed an observed shift in Robbie's demeanor and her mouth convulsed in shrieks of accusations as Wyndam moved one lumpy brown pea across the striped saucer of his place steaming with uneaten starches.

Wyndam told his buddy, Alfonso at the car shop in Jersey, about Dolly and how he just couldn't help himself. For weeks he didn't sleep before he fucked her and he still didn't sleep afterward, Wyndam explained, knotting his hairy knuckles on the glossy red hood of a car in the dingy fluorescent light of the garage. Gizmos hammering and bolts whining, the occasional laugh and portable radio reality discussion clustering in the recesses of darkness. Alfonso told Wyndame to take some of his own medicine, lithium was never unkind.

Scorpio Fernandez worked in a flat above St. Mark's Theater on the corner. Fourth floor, last door on the left, it all took place in those walls where the light from a candle flickered on a wall, thrown down towards the floor littered with conical shaped contraptions that held the flesh in a rapture of humiliation. Scorpio Fernandez left the kitchen after pouring more rum. She lowered her peaked cap with a chain above her delicately arched blonde brow, brushing the rubber tip of her jack boot on the tin bowl of cat food by the dishwasher, opening her long leather trench coat as she smoked.

"Be there eventually you piece of shit" She called out.

It's all one big performance. Scorpio Fernandez didn't start here, twirling a riding crop by her pudgy bare white thigh, the remnants of a torn stocking clinging to her kneecap. She placed her gloved black hand on the thumb cuffs of her patron, probing their tightness, before a padlock was adjusted to the suspended harness from the ceiling, briefly smiling at his helpless vulnerability.

"It's humiliating to have to humiliate a pig like you" Scorpio Fernandez whispered as she drank more rum and placed a clothespin on his nose and lips. Saliva peeking out of the corner of his mouth in a fizzy white glob.

Scorpio Fernandez liked to shift from cold to hot, starting with ice cubes and ending with wax. She was a pro-domme to the most enticing degree of debasement. She loved her hogties fastened on the ankles. It was a performance, one-night nurse, one-night cop, maintained her reputation as the dominatrix with the berry pink nipples that protruded from her black leather catsuit that shimmered like the moon on a river.

Most of her clients were the business type. Conservatives looking for their fascist mother. Pin striped vests on discount after Christmas. They had the money and the time to enter the lair of Scorpio Fernandez and ask for a flogging with her toes jutting in their mouths and urethral play gone gentle their desire for golden showers on the balcony before the roar of traffic, bustling to a cosmic irrelevance. Squeezing their biceps with a playful skepticism, their endorphins spiked out of their scalps, wanting to be taken down and told about their subsequent irresponsibility, derived from a tidy stepmother and chapel dean.

Scorpio Fernandez took pleasure in providing the nausea and elicit ultimatums to her johns, preferably ones she knew from the coffee shop she worked in with a flaccid balding Greek entrepreneur, beneath the drawbridge near Aldini. A mafia cuisine serving salmon on fire in the pan on the table. She used to hustle for Sal in the metro by the bay, gray tides threaded with white like the distillation of a vacant room, the equation to a sooth midlife crisis in handcuffs and CBT. Coke could strike to save her pain on solitary nights, leaning into the armoire, finger a tattoo and a scar someone printed in her spine with a needle, plunging into the want, plunging into the serenity of elation, giving herself away.

She used to hustle for Sal, he once ground a cigar into the back of her hand. His grizzled paw snaked between the crevice of her cleft ass, smoothing liquor down the skin. Her torso was marked with a bloody crescent. Crooked teeth. She was his animal, posed in shackles on a bed, redundant in her moaning of how pitiful and pointless her conception was.

Scorpio Fernandez was not the victim anymore, gagged pale on a teal carpet of a motel. *Fuck me like mom.* Begging for the love she couldn't give herself. Before she quit, she began to visit a psychiatrist referred by her case worker.

She began seeing her psychiatrist twice a week and every time she entered his office she was overwhelmed by surrender, divulging details of her decay without remorse or content. All her life, from the back door of the house on the corner where Sissy lived, making love to her pot-bellied father who never cared, stepping into the club on South in nipple tassels and stilettos that could poke a hole in any heart as flammable and disposable as hers. She had sessions with the psychiatrist at eight, his last appointment block, because she was always late and he was always tired. Eventually the psychiatrist became enthralled by her descriptions of torture. Trembling over her rhetoric about the way you could make a man shiver if you placed a finger on the right nerve, and how sometimes at night she cradled her calves to her chest and longed for meaning. Longing for security that would never find her, pissed away like the money splayed across her navel, slick with a pasty ejaculation.

Eventually Scorpio Fernandez discovered she had no clothes and her psychiatrist had draped his tie over his shoulder as he fucked her, jabbing desperately. Grunting and fuming profanities, biting his bottom lip and turning his face to the pock-marked ceiling. *And where is your hypothesis about my anger now? Tell me the best coping strategies.*

Lust was the platelet in the stream of blood pulsing in her arms, skinned with alienation, Wyndam Gray, her psychiatrist, unbuttoned his shift and articulated notions of commitment and discretion. Perhaps Wyndam doubted Scorpio Fernandez's abyss, had forgotten how she could withstand the penetrating glares. Wyndam told her of his insomnia, his current inability to please his wife and the financial migraines. She wanted Wyndam even as she told him her sins; she wanted someone who could hold her secrets and sustain some of the damage for her. Likely to pause on the cliff.

Scorpio Fernandez transitioned from beaten to punisher. The lime nylon thong and multiple zippered corset was just an accessory to her demise, a companion clinging to her ribcage as she lashed and reprimanded. Giving some answer to their existence, some religious zeal about how they were born bad and she saw every second.

Had she been born for such trysts? Was she bred to dominate? Could the pain be anymore assimilated to her childish temperament? Answers left her nothing but resignation, she pleaded for inquiries that diffused and disarmed the subtle rage humming behind a lonesome stare in a flat.

Scorpio Fernandez received a reservation for a single white male at seven. Scorpio Fernandez thrilled at the flourishing list of clients she received, some intern must have mentioned her talent passed on man by man like chlamydia in a school yard.

After Scorpio placed her crotchless hot pants over the back of the back, she sighed while running her chapped pale hands down her smooth exfoliated face. Scorpio had begun to look to her clients with an expectation, formulating her own philosophy about the reproductive instincts of civilization. She was expecting the doorbell any minute as she sat in the magenta loveseat, perfecting the outline of her mauve lipstick.

Five minutes later, Scorpio Fernandez answered the door, using a voice box that radiated a distant allure like the residue of a bourbon bottle.

"Hey, you're my seven, aren't you?"

"My name's Robbie" he began, shuffling on the doormat. He wore a blue sweater with denims creased in anticipating cheapness, Scorpio frowned. "I am Wyndam Gray's son. I want you to do everything to me that you did to my father" Robbie placed the money on the crotch of his jeans.

"I don't know if I can do this" she muttered

"You're a professional. I'm a professional."

Scorpio Fernandez quietly agreed as she unbuttoned her frock, "You're just as bad as he was"

"I'm not afraid to feel"

It began in the covert stages of psychiatry and no other exit was as narrow and claustrophobic as her heart. Hate is for the hag in latex.

Island of Loss

Morning comes in the same strike of light on the veranda, gliding into the living room. The love in my heart is pounding and pointless. Triggering laughs like a storm of napalm from the sky. Raining from heaven in radioactive sprays and penetrating the shadows of this forest, the shadows of this island I have found myself on. Far from home and forever in debt to its mild climate and elusive migrant traveling up the mountain like a widow in rags with a bundle of sticks, glaring down the dirt road as the sun settles on the whaling boats a mile out.

The lighthouse stands on the east of the island, a mile from the town where emergency kits and chicken dinners are in the same lot. Parceled on a cart by the butcher in his apron, speckled with the black dried drops of blood from the counter with a scale and a cleaver. Eyeing the crowd like an old hound, his milky blue eyes flickering across the stands.

There's a post off two miles from the bay, beside a damp school house church including an arthritic academic in orthopedic shoes and pencil skirt. Children congregate in the movie house at dusk, the floor littered with the remains of caramel popcorn, scattered around their teeth like rotting teeth.

The whore house by the hardware store has been abandoned since Lunatic Lorelai died and left all her cash to the orphans of X, the cottage she lived in as a child that left her malnourished and entitled to some pity. The prostitutes left the island for Madrid and Tel Aviv, hopping ships with plum leather suitcases; the frayed edges of an indigo scarf trailing on the black planks of the dock. Into the new life, into the new world, out of the asylum of their past discontent and out of the enraged satin mattress that squealed through the walls like an unhinged nerve.

I've lived in a cabin since last spring. In the winter the snow falls like a veil smothering critters and cowards in their lairs and blinding the caves with crystal spears. Silencing the midday prayers father's parched pink mouth pressed in my ears from a boyhood casualty, the faith in a deity dwindling in the whirlpool of adolescence, he and I grew distant. His words never left me, the verses that I never cherished as he did, slid past my eyes and into my hands I cupped over my face, washing away the loneliness.

The island was my escape but it proved to be a perpetrator of alienation. I used to walk the mountain and sit on boulders outside the forest, gazing down at the glassy silhouette of the town. The twinkling beams of the lighthouse bursting through the fog, touching a vacant pasture in me that raised my palpitations to a deafening score, spiritual compromise to the island. Eternity was a void as easily comprehended as a minute and I could live more in an hour than a decade if I counted the seasons of my infidelities in Cologne and Istanbul. I am a flawed gentleman, as most, but I do believe in war and insanity, rather than some flushed apostle. I should have sacrificed my adventures for the succor, a wife and a toast brick household, because the booze ran out. I'm not longer a delirious lubricated clown but a sincerely pathetic vehicle of repressed ideologies about the love I gave in a flat and the wine I fermented in a cellar jar like a transcended panic, asking to be tasted and appreciated by my petrified tongue.

In November I left the cabin to partake in my habitual walk through the forest. The birds were heard but not seen, a poisonous squawking fled from the trees in a scuffle of leaves. Pine needs circling the base of a tree and a subtle ray of daylight measuring itself out in hourly praises down the path, lighting my loins with a simple inebriation.

There was a loaf of bread under my arm and a sack on my back containing various utensils, a deck of cards, a pocket lighter. The air felt muggy plastered thick on my skin of moss and fern. I broke my arm three years ago in a car accident and it still stings to carry a shovel and mend a fence, but I am growing accustomed to such pangs of soreness and expect no change.

I followed my path up the mountains, each step became more labored than the previous and the incline tugged on my blood pressure. I sat on a soggy log crawling with emerald colored beetles and a buzzard twitched in the soil, fertile clay. I would have eaten my loaf but I was saving it for a secluded area beyond the path where I could rest my heels on a stump and listening for the rumbling of the railroad far away, carriers thundering down rails in an industrial intrusion to this solitude.

As I began walking once more, wiping my brow with a tanned arm, I grew dizzy upon a rotting smell that confronted me at the cave and intensified as I traveled farther up the path. The smell tasted like bad ham, offering a sick decay that was closer than I wanted to believe. My boot hit the skull and I swore it wasn't there, swore it wasn't what I thought it would be. That maybe I'd just started to go mad instead.

There was no death on this island, untouched by the world and its sorrows. How could such ghastly instincts of destruction find themselves a home in my utopian mountain side? How did they find me here when it was all so far away?

Her corpse was beautiful if you believed in that sort of afterlife that lingers in the features delicate like an Aryan snowfall, blond tendrils under earlobes, bloated cheeks slanting her eyes. Her hands were tied in a sailor's knot and her magenta velvet pumps caked with mud. Her legs had been shaven smooth and the maggots hadn't burrowed in those ample pores, distinguished by the roundness of her calves and knobby knees of a schoolgirl. She was one of Lunatic Lorelei's whore who never escaped the island. Some sailor must have found her in the deli, fingering the lettuce and cherry tomatoes with a soothing calculation of ripeness. Her rigor mortis silver eye shadow drooped sideways and a collapsed esophagus, adorned in a gold chain with a diamond shaped locket, tarnished with funereal ambiguity.

She was beautiful even in decomposition and it made me sad to see such a damsel gone to waste in the mud. How could he leave such fineries for the insects? She was so damned beautiful. Wish I'd had the luck to dive her muff in a motel or bite her thighs and hear some moan so thoroughly imprinted with her own vulnerability.

O how good she must have tasted once. O how relaxing it must have been to cradle her in your arms as you slept. She was dead and I had found her, like nobody else had. Her legs splayed and her silk nightgown patterned with dull violets, clinging to her muscles like tissue, translucent and ghostly like her gaze. It would have been a sweet joy to know her alive I'm sure.

I could not leave her. Found myself sitting by her side reciting these observations of her inherent beauty. Sympathized with her, unlike I had when my terrier, Mondo, died before I could take him to the countryside to visit Mama and her empty house filled with wax dolls and china plates, commenting on my thinness like a sin. A scrutiny I accepted with maternal fondness unlike my father.

It was by her in the forest, left for nothing, partial to moonlight and moths rather than harsh parallels of sun that I named her Diana. It was easier to talk to her then.

I began to dream about making love to Diana and gave her a history of siblings and attributes. I gave her a personality. Perfectly calm and complacent with thoughts on whether to touch her face and ask her if she was an angel that fell to earth for me to find in the gothic quarries of indifference. She brought out my fire and stoked the flame in her passivity, and I was surprised to admit we were friends.

Every day I would visit Diana. Bag a sandwich and hurry from the cabin, straightening my posture and offering hymns of devotion and fear. I was afraid to be in love with a corpse, but on the island, nobody seemed to notice her disappearance. My advantage. Our secrecy excited me when I was alone. Ashamed by my erection, upon picturing her hands, inflexible and pale, and I could kiss a thousand times and never feel at ease. I wanted Diana, I told her about my life and my philosophies, and she listened, gaining a comfort I never had, something I couldn't live without anymore, and I was never happier. I looked forward to visiting her every day and even built a shrine around her decaying corpse of rosemary and dandelions. A floral vignette of her frame that I celebrated by dancing naked under the moon with a hand on my scepter and a torch in my heart.

If Diana could live for only one day, if that delinquent sailor had not taken her, I could have waltzed with her, pressed her body against mine in the darkness and briefly suffocated the pain that had no more boundaries in my life, plaguing and paralyzing me. O the sensation of my eruption in the abrasive mahogany walls of the cabin, thinking of my valor and her blossomed eroticism, electrifying my veins and sustaining a dream I could never hope for.

She was my savior and I prayed for her apparition in dreams. I loved Diana like someone I never had, and the sadness was not a fear anymore. I didn't wake each morning with the fear of surviving my melancholy. I could live again in the fantasy and orgasm in quiet singularity in the wretches of my cabin. Biding the hours to my tardy demise. To join her.

One evening I could no longer stand myself and I was so overwhelmed I packed a butcher knife from the kitchen drawer in my knapsack beside the volume of Years I had packed in worship of her beauty. My maiden sleeps in the forest but I can still visit her, before the worms digest greater parts of her anatomy and I am left again by the desperation of this island, pushing me aside in its seclusion, inviting me with her flesh I longed to taste. I have never heard her voice and this bothers me deeply on some nights, but I do not let it insist in my head.

When I found Diana that evening a bear had been dining on her shoulder. I screamed and removed my butcher knife from my sack, an expulsion of air from my lungs of the most insatiate odium. The animal snickered at me and strolled away. I sighed upon the damage.

I was traumatized by her stillness then. This increasing sensation of loss and helplessness. I had to have something to remember her by, some artifact of her anatomy before it surrendered to nature's cycle of degradation. Where would I go without Diana? Placed in my heart and killing me slowly with her brow. Nobody understands the detrimental sensitivity of poets. Removed the butcher knife from my sack and placed a hand on her crotch, pulling down her panties and plunging the steel inside her. Longing for the vibrant blood, the bitter coolant, to carry me across the final passage in my tormented soul. I cut up Diana like the butcher in town, without remorse but driven by a passionate route into the sacred temples of her flesh, begging for me and I begging for it. After maneuvering the butcher knife and taking multiple calculations about the diameter of her labia minora, I cut out her clitoris and ate it quietly beside her. Paid no attention to the rot it bestowed, swallowing her skin succulent and soft in my mouth, the bulb tickling my tonsils with its pubic ingenuity. Perversion and desecration were farthest from my mind as I tasted her, finally like I had a dreamt a million nights alone in the darkness, desiring a fulfillment that could finally silence my lust. She was as delectable as I hoped, and my mouth hurt for more.

I buried Diana after that. Gave her sanctity and made a headstone from bark. I carved her name and mine. Someone would look upon it and roll their eyes like we were teenagers. I wonder if she could see how loved she was by me. It does not matter, for the tumult of time would cease to name such syllables as mine. Diana was a starlet in my opium-fractured eye. She is gone now, beneath the earth where she belongs, and I do not wish for her presence anymore. She was good enough as she was and I don't want to feel anymore.

Desire is the marrow in my spine, snap me cold and bitter with treason. As a necrophiliac saint I am not ashamed I plead for her touch and cry in the night wishing I wasn't so complicated. But touch me the same, please.

You reach out to me but I am not a person anymore. Like groping for an unlit candle in complete darkness. For the night is long and the road is hard but I fear no failures. I fear nothing except the peripheral fantasies of Diana, a neural parasite. My fantasy that never sleeps, never wakes, unafraid and irresponsible for the inevitability of time.

Edge of Life

*T*hank *you, thank you.* Inestia Croalow blushed into her cashmere frock, an old gift Lionel had set before her under the Christmas tree eight years ago. Before the illness took him and frightened us all away. Inestia Croalow rubbed her ear, sore from the mini microphone hooked under her jaw, hidden in a thin silky white fret of hair. The interview was completed. Just finished the final interview she was granting the public, tugging on a martini and smiling at the reporter on the satin sofa across from her. *You did really well Inestia, it was such a pleasure to meet you.*

Inestia Croalow was abducted by a band of teenage militia once and hypnotized into loving her captor, Marcandro Stignotovish. She muttered their solemn promises of bloodshed and shook her fists before a super8 in a basement, plucked down on the dusty cement floor, chained to a wall. One bucket for waste, one for water. That was thirty-seven years ago, before Inestia was rescued and punched into a state ward for six years. Later she lived a quiet life with Lionel and two petite ferociously petty dogs. Becoming the author of a poignant, harrowing, heartbreaking memoir that shot her into the public eye. For some time, she occupied a seat of mystery; the victim of a sabotaged youth, taken into the hand that crushed and deforms minds to its agenda.

The thorns of light hovered above her, saddling her cheekbones in a radiant spark of cosmetics. A drowsy murmur escaped that thin wide mouth, watching conversations around her from set employees cleave and sunder. They filtered from the room, dragging cables and steel cases out of the foyer. All of them envied Inestia, a woman who inherited her fame from a coincidental hostage. Inestia did not have to work, mire in any disappointed dreams and scrape and claw her potential to the sunlight. She is a refugee of her own will, the pucker and swell of abject horror.

Her beloved Lionel canned in the hideous bakelite urn above the fireplace spoke aloud to her. *You're only an oddity to these parasites. They lock into you like a morsel of decay, they know you're old and you may die, so they're chasing this month's ratings. You're faded, Inestia, faded.*

"Shut the fuck up, Lionel!" she yelled into the empty room and sobbed. These sobs came onto her like a column of cold air and lingered for hours. Curling her into an animal on the couch, shaking toward an indestructible world of the past. Inestia lifted her bleary eyes to the window, observing the gray crust of snow at the base of a tree bearded in lichen. Her mind returned to her childhood, of Philadelphia in the summer heat and her father's fruit stand on South Street. One solitary image remains of Inestia's childhood, before being seized by Marcandro Stignotovich. A crate of bananas baking on the sidewalk in July sun.

A jackal's fang winked in the corner of the room. A grim heart clenched in ice, living on the edge of life.

"I'm fascinated by you" the man said, stepping away from the door hinge toward her chair before slouching into the satin sofa the reporter previously warmed. His hands were thick and red, woodcutting thumbs. Hands with a mossy web of black hair on the backs that ran through his smoke curls knit tender and shiny to his scalp. A tuft of hair fell into his lap and he noticed Inestia protracting her gaze to the carpet.

"As you can see I've aged like you" Tickled by his own wisdom, he smiled a deep wide hatred.

"Who are you?" she whispered, her seat molding around her body, breathing monitored and measured.

"Don't hurt my feelings. Think hard. And not about yourself. Remember when you arrived in the ward? And you were jabbering nonsense?"

Inestia tried, shaking her brain for loose change. She thought of the ward, big hefty men hooked around her. An orderly pet her head and she bit him, snaking back to a clipboard near his desk. Name? Birthday? Blood type? History of mental illness? Questions chattered at the officers around her, clinging to the walls in a hastened thought, slow to answer for Inestia as she rolled her eyes about, clouded. The ward and its superb specialty in devouring dignity, fled from Inestia. The jackal frowned, disappointed. But he also relished in it, he had the power.

"I am your aborted son. I am your angel of death"

Inestia cackled with unreasonable enthusiasm, a deranged bat pleading for glitch. She sprang from her chair and pointed to the door. He scoffed and patted the space on the sofa beside him, were those tears she thought she saw?

"Please, mother. Let me be with you"

"Don't call me that!" She gazed to Lionel's urn. Lionel, her hero, redefined the romantic love her captors planted in her. She nursed him into the narrow cell of his death, into a pillowed wooden womb. A net of smoke looped around her as she stood, lassoing her into the sofa.

Inestia looked into the eyes of this strange man, burning with a quick impulse to eat her. She found herself skidding across these bleak waters, shivering in their candid openness. They begged to be coddled, the eyes oblivious as a newborn. *Don't listen to him,* Lionel's urn repeated.

But did Inestia want to live? Such a magical egress proposed by an intruder grew more charming.

"Why are you my angel of death?

"Everyone's individual angel of death is a person they betrayed in this life"

A riddle of disagreement pursed Inestia's lips. Motherhood is a choice. A swirl of rage engulfed Inestia, and her frail paper hands rested on each cheek of the angel.

"You are no angel. You are an agent of the devil."

The man chewed the inside of his cheeks, he lowered his eyes to her finger tips placed on his stubble. Intrigued by hands that never stroked him, hands that never handled his woes with supreme clarity and fatigue. An isolated pause, Inestia felt the blood draining from her hands. Clotting, tangling, tightening and releasing, racing up her arms into her chest.

If one entered the room the following day, all to be seen, was a silver cap of hair protruding from the lip of a sofa.

Lola 23

Been in this hospital too long. Too long under sheets, subdued and immobilized with legs amputated from the crash and burns on sixteen percent of his body. The pilot, Z. Stetson was a coltish giant removed and now resides paralytic and palsied in a pharmacopeia called *hospital*. This hospital is located somewhere on Saturn, closer to the burnished bulbs of moons and stars that shimmer like shattered glass in smoke.

No legs. Insides black from the toxic smoke in the ship he was flying. The ship was a flaming eagle of space spiraling down into a black blind void. Swallowed like a moth in oil. His shallow breaths reflect some contrived enthusiasm to improve, he coughs like he's choking back anthracite. His voice that was once sonorous and reassuring is stripped to an incipient grunt. Whispers conjured with the greatest anxiety. He can't even begin to explain his sexual starvation. It's absolutely terrifying. He's been reduced to some cursory onanism when the lights are low and the talking has stopped.

Z. Stetson, Captain Stetson, Commander of KI-34. Infusion of pilot, technician, military protege, diplomatic corpuscle. He's been in the hospital for three months, but he does not know this. Stetson's memory has been impaired from a brain hemorrhage in the crash. Wife and child unrecognized as indistinct buzzards of a family unit. The pilot's wife, Stetson's mate he cannot recall, and Esteria Winifred, is dead.

He's failed to recall any shred of sympathy for his marriage. The doctors presented pictures of Stetson's family to him and their grinning freckled faces went unnoticed. The rippling screen of an image aching with love muted, severed from his conscious attachments. Stetson was an adultery yet all the rooftop parties he fawned over his wife and whined pathetic madrigals of praise to her beauty. Esteria Winifred with that meretricious flare. Inept in virtues like tact or kindness yet intimidating into admiration with the lucidity in her stark bluntness. Stetson was captivated by the lacquered shiver of her sweaty back, smoke coiling around her ears from a post-coital cigarette.

During his three months stay at the space hospital, Stetson went through three nurses. Robot nurses of the sleekest chrome designated to separate wings and patrolling halls. Humans are doctors and administrators while robots are nurses and custodians.

Nurses were granted white dresses zipped up the back and caps to give them a more embracing, human quality. Their humming chests and twitching shoulder lacked any semblance of casualness. Most deliberate in the same monotone contralto murmur. Sometimes Stetson watched these robot nurses as their sterile arctic steel fingertips wrapped his stumps.

Three nurses in three months resigned their shift to Stetson's unit. He confused the robots, threw food, shoved, spat, and screamed. Abused the robot nurses and damned their botched imitations of empathy. The latest robot nurse was spattered with feces and wires ripped from the back of her neck, between the metal rods connecting the steel skull and aluminum vertebrae. Stetson earned the reputation as the most treacherous patient in the ward. No leg Stetson, embittered and barbaric as he grabbed at the silvery elbows of his nurses. Their sweet ward.

The hospital board held multiple meetings regarding the abhorrent tendencies of Stetson. They feared his psychological as well as physical recovery from the shattered filament of his previous life. They were informed of his neurotic irritation and depressing denial of his wife and family. If the evening peeled out according to pre-prandial clipboard agenda, he was sedated. Meds often spat out. Ritual morphine infection gave a thirsted fever by dawn.

With thorough research, the hospital board advised a scheme. The board retrieved pictures of Stetson's late wife, the Esteria Winifred, and created a robot with features and hair color nearly identical to her. Though Stetson did not remember his wife, the hospital board hoped the robot would be a subconscious salve to him. They model the robot's posture, wardrobe, complexion after a license photo they retrieved from the drifts of a federal database.

The resemblance was petrifying, if not engaging. Even the doctors, human doctors with spectacles and dry skin, were aroused by the Esteria-copy robot. She was the twenty third robot produced at the facility that year, titled Lola 23. Instead of hands as metallic clutches they were insulated in fleshy pale nodes. She even had plastic pink toenails and subtle pearl earrings.

The Lola 23 was introduced in March. She entered Stetson's room. A slinky demure brunette. There was no plausible grief when Lola 23 approached.

Her coral lips formed words in the softest polished tempo. Her shoulders were sweet fruit. A fatal gesture like the purr of a forehead-kiss or a forearm-pat spun Stetson into prismatic fantasy. Left his brain wobbling in its scalp. A mere friction of her blouse against his biceps struck his heart into a convulsion of joy. The hospital board was beyond thrilled, they were exasperated with glee.

Lola 23 was patient and joking to Stetson's advances. His chilling needy appeals were responded with the same polite chirps she uttered when she detected danger. *No, sir. I don't understand, sir. Please explain for me, sir.* Her composure remained undisturbed and fluid. Details that didn't have any particular relevance crawled inside his veins as he slept. Details like the naked convex of her forehead to the puckering dimples in her cheeks.

Myriad blessings crammed in his brow, trembling with an exclusive motive to inhabit the dusty metallic cavity of Lola 23 with his wretched need. The ataxia of wretched need. Need with no other avenue to express its deviance, spoken in human language and offensive to ears untrained in reproductive formalities.

The skin of her wrist weighing on his collar and does he ask for everything? Does he ask for time at least once, bid hid favor, and spare him? He asks to be bathed by her, for poppies to infuriate his bloodstream with paranormal tranquility. He asks to be silenced, pulse steadied, rotten and filthy.

Lola 23 sailed into the room and lowered a tray at the foot of his bed.

"Chicken sandwich" she pinged.

"Lola, I need you to say something for me"

"Yes, sir?"

"I need you to tell me you love me. All I want to hear is you love me."

"I cannot, sir. I am not programmed to do so"

Citadel Insanity

Starting at the beginning is an excuse for my present. Starting at the end is an excuse for my past. I didn't start in the womb or grade school, and I didn't end in my backyard, aloof and forlorn. It's the gap. I'm not a chronological device. A memory without phases. Clips and cuts, hairs of a second, fractions of a minute that mean more than any swath of time. I am the beginning and the end, and you were my middle I started for and finished without.

Bobby Claudshaw's birthday party was Sunday. Memorial Day I was on a train from Peach Hill Behavioral Unit with a gangrene soul knifed by glances and whispers. Voices stopped muttering when shocks came. Headaches increased. Strapped to a platform, mouth gear to keep my tongue away from my teeth. The bleeding fist of my heart repeating, *I'm a man, I'm a man.*

Before my collapse I was a mathematician. I was hailed as a genius, miracle to mankind. Awards, ribbons, trophies, cocktail parties, promotions, petty suits, buckled trousers, crescent spectacles, house keys, electric bill. Inanimate continuum. On top of the world. Spilled my insides on ice, got loud with some cowards. Found myself naked in a rainstorm jumping on the hoods of cars and crowning the parking lot with my flaccid member.

They said the time away would do me good. Lithium, electric convulsions, hypodermic needles, flea pillow case, urine stained linoleum, plastic ashtrays, and pajamas dusty and washed away of color like the inside of bone, would do me good. Real good. A good I've never had before in my life. A good that would change me into a better man. A good that wouldn't harm myself or others. A good that could take out the pain and replace it with ethical praise. A good that would rag me from the gutters of citadel insanity, to dream normal things we all could laugh about.

I could not explain why I was there, what grew against my chest cavity and why it kept persisting, long through day, long through hour, long through season. I could sparsely articulate, who are you, why did you get here, do you still want your life back? No. I don't want the academic pedigree anymore, indoctrination and salvation in the satisfaction of salary, tenure, time table speculation. I don't want that man who was screaming naked.

I'm not looking for joy. I'm looking not to lie awake alone in bed with my hands on my throat and toes tucked under bars. I'm not looking to the sunrise, to the moonlight, to the leaves skittering down the street and maple trunks crystallized in dew. I'm looking to stay alive.

I'm looking to survive myself. Looking back and sick with grief. Looking back with melancholy at my mask of stability. Looking back with a keen twinkle in my cornea. Looking at myself, towel dry, perfumed with blood, looking on at dusk with proud euphoria. Another day undead.

Bobby Claudshaw turned ten the first week of June and the birthday party would be held in their backyard with scotch for the fathers and iced lemon tea for the kids. Drinking has been out of my orbit some months. I like a thimble of peace. Since I came home I've been living with my parents and I feel like a teenager again. They tried to instill a curfew but that's humiliating for a fifty-two-year-old man.

My mother pulled me into this prepubescent birthday party because she thought I might mingle with the divorced hags but I find their dogs more attractive than their pimpled ass cheeks. The husbands are discussing car brands and various routes they took to arrive here. Talking manly things like horse races, dry walls, and holiday bonuses. Talking about professions, taxes, baseball stadiums, and actresses dripping with elicit amniotic profundity. The men can spot my crooked thoughts a mile away and know to steer clear of my gaze, and they know not to offer me a handshake under the pinstriped awning.

Instinct says I'm a lunatic that should be left for nature's extermination, whether by my own hand or an authority. Don't blame them, I'd be frightened of my specimen if it crawled onto my property and dined in a playhouse near my kid. I'm contagious. My negative perspective oozes through casual acquaintance. Don't care for boundaries, never quite enforced them in myself. Don't care for quality or predictability, I've accepted my erratic paradox.

Everyone was outside on the back patio near a trampoline. A helium tank knocked over and rainbow balloons were tied to the grill. Reclining in a lime green beach chair, I twitched my feet to a tune from the radio and my mother was cackling louder than anybody, even the newlyweds huddled close by were uncomfortable. My mother's laugh makes up for the both of us. I remember as a kid we'd go to the movies and every punchline tickled her. She'd shift in her chair and stick her tongue between her teeth and hiss with amusement until all the sound waves fucked her bridgework. That laugh came back. It burst onto the pavement like fireworks, forcing people to turn.

Emptying my tumbler and sucking the venom from my gums while anticipating a yawn, I walked away from the crowd into the house. Birthday cake hoisted over their heads and little Bobby Claudshaw danced.

In the house I walked down the hall, observing the family portraits. The stone-faced father with the supple bride enclosed in white. The baby swaddled in wool. The terrier with a deer leg. First grade picture day, missing front teeth and cosmic doubt. Bach arose, scooped my sadness out of my ears and filled them with ultimate calm, and then worse, insatiable curiosity. Strutting down the hall with a palm on the wallpaper, sandy and dry against my skin, the piano was louder. Parting a door, I saw a girl, arms wavering above keys and head tilted towards sheets spread on a shelf.

I entered the room and leaned against the wall, accidentally nudging a painting frame with my shoulder. You finished your piece and I cleared my throat. You turned around, your freckled cheeks flush with surprise, again I cleared my throat.

"How did you get in here?" you asked, curling your hands in your lap and kicking the pedal of the piano. The dingey haze of the lamp scattered shadows on the carpet.

"I followed the music. It was great. I wanted to be here up close for the end"

You said nothing, lowered your chin to your chest and fingered the lace hem of your pale green sun dress. Your knees were sunburned and a birthmark the size of a dime was exposed on the shin. You were young. Young enough only to have blonde fuzz on your thighs and flat buds on your chest. High school acne was a year away, your innocent furrowed brow as you bit your lip was like watching a flower perplexed with sun, you were endless and untouched.

"What's your name?" I asked, shaking the ice in my glass, attempting to appear bored.

"Inez Claudshaw"

"How old are you? You're really talented for someone so young"

"Thirteen" She tucked a crimped brown lock behind her pink ear, unpierced.

"How come you're not outside at the party? Don't you want to wish your brother a happy birthday?"

"No, I don't like people"

"Me too"

Pass me over, I thought. Pass me right by. I can taste my own sickness. Overcome with an embarrassed identification I withdrew from the room. Overcome with a strange wonder, ask me to unleash my libido on your tight angelic openness. The hospital thought they stunned the savage out of my skill, but it breathes and eats daffodils like you. You avoided my stare.

After Bobby Claudshaw's birthday I watched you from the second story window as you hung sheets in your backyard, folded flannel in a wicker basket and wiped your hands on your legs. I watched with hate for the oblivious way you bounced between lawn chairs. I wanted to rescue you from myself. I waited with a fast illusion.

Waiting till three, I'd sit on my porch and count the minutes till you, Inez Claudshaw, passed with your school bag. Scathed by your hesitation to greet me, I waved. In my room I fell to my knees, fell for your quiet deities, fell for the sky absent of clouds and populated with your hormonal intensity.

Halloween was coming and summer's blush burned out to autumn's severe landscapes. Shook myself reckless with notions of right and wrong. I've lost my hope and fear.

I was at your bus stop. My hands were in my pocket. You asked me how I was. So mature for your age.

"I'm great, I'm great" I repeated to convince myself.

"I'm not that great. Just tired. You know how it is"

"I do know how it is" I reassured her, cupping her shoulder with my right hand, walking down the sidewalk, the orb of my entire being diffusing in a yoke of mild annoyance. I followed you to your front lawn and asked you to take a walk with me.

"Um-okay. But not long I have homework"

"Sure. Don't worry about it" I said, scratching my jaw and eyeing an open window of her house.

Cars whirred past us.

The welts decorating your shoulders were landmines of my despair, crying out to the trees I asked you to care. Stop crying, you're too old for that.

They are still looking for you. It's an unusual headline. Mathematician severs lips from flawless face of thirteen-year-old girl. I'm shaken, shaken to the foundation for formulas that will not explain why I chose you. I'm searching for the base of my debasement. I picked you because you were the one alone in the house, away from the others and destined for solitude like me. You lured me. My fantasies are my only friends. If the days were short and the night peeled out the moonlight like melon rinds. If only the jungle of my wants would sleep. Running from the asylum that has my name carved on their forefinger.

Days evolve into weekends and holidays. I pray for your parents, fingering their cheap blinds thinking they heard your voice on the lawn. Looking for you to come bounding down the asphalt. Last call for these feelings that never go away.

I pray for planetary indifference to your disappearance. I remember crouching over you in the grass, burning with calculating criminal impulse.

Visions of Infinity

First three, receding hairline, paunch swung over an elastic waistband. Rudiger was laid off four months ago by the power plant, a common plight of the recession. Since he didn't have a wife or family to support, the corporation saw little potential in his extensive sideburns and thumb blisters. AARP sent him pamphlets every month with smiling octogenarians, their dentures glinting in the sunlight.

Rudiger's friend was a man named Weston who lived in the apartment across the hall. They worked together at the power plant but Weston was fifteen years younger and had two children so he kept his job. He smelled like Listerine and tobacco with a laugh that wound up in his chest like a fire alarm. His living room was littered with dolls missing arms and heads. Rudiger admired this recognition of the human body's fragility, articulated by the angry hands of Weston's five-year-old daughter.

"It's just a phase" Antoinette, Weston's wife, explained while placing a chalky red hand on the wall. Antoinette had cold sores and eyebrows plucked like stitches.

"Do you believe in second lives?" Rudiger asked Weston one night while playing cards together, Antoinette at the laundromat. Weston folded his arms and lit his cigarette.

"Why, you want another one?" Weston replied, winking at his daughter who was kicking a block across the carpet. The little girl must have sensed a shift in the atmosphere because she sat down in front of the television and stared at the men. A curtain of light flickering on one side of her face.

"In a second life, I'd be normal," Rudiger said, listening to the radiator on the other side of the room.

"I thought you agreed we were in this together?" Weston asked, trying to be charismatic, "The other night Antoinette started screaming in bed."

"How come?"

"She said she felt Panther"

Panther was Antoinette's beloved black cat that died four months ago. It stopped eating and started shitting on the couch. Weston explained that

Antoinette felt Panther's ghost crawl between them in bed.

"That's a damn shame" Rudiger could only say.

In the apartment, half past four am, when the bottles stopped breaking the street outside, Rudiger strolled through his bedroom examining his jars.

Abortion fetish. Each jar had an unborn child inside. He could stick himself in the jar and marinate himself. Standing there by the window sill, brushing himself alone their cold lifeless faces like poking pale stones.

Collection of rejection, he accumulated the unborn accomplishments and infinite possibilities of several lifetimes. He liked thinking about the chrome clamps on tissue paper, a rubber glove squeaking with blood, the chamber of a syringe emptied. Their hands crystallized in a bent formation. Cast away by their parents, he was their father now.

On his lunch breaks, Weston left the power plant for the hospital where he stalked the halls and visited people while they slept. Anyone asked, he was a distant relative. Cancer patient fetish, he purged his lust on powder blue bed sheets. He was erect when he saw someone with a shaved head, even more enthralled if they were ashen and bony. Once Weston watched a woman with breast cancer undress and the hollow bruises on her chest were like fisted craters in dough. Once an old man with lung cancer awoke and spay gooey sepia phlegm that landed on Weston's wrist as he jerked himself. Once a little girl with leukemia cried herself to sleep and Weston sat on her bed half an hour naked.

If the men could accept each other. Maybe they could accept themselves.

Man in Sand

This is his hut. A ramshackle of patched cedar shingles on the edge of the land, on a muggy pier. The hut leans back away from the sea, bent towards the western winds that urge back to a paradise long gone. A clang of seagulls whirl around the roof, plucking worms from the gutters. His hut steams silver troughs of light in the winter, a small fire warming his bunions and cooking mackerel and the like. The floor of the hut is littered with dirty clothes, fabric stitched together from Ma back home before the war, before she was killed for harboring a deserter and he fled to the sea. Into the arms of this sea. The waves tumbling into land and mists of salt erode the painted door. He spent his first day here searching for sea shells along the embankment glaring and slapping through the sharp ginger stems of weeds under the pier. Finding no shells to sell to the mainland, only fragments of clam shells, some split like the snarled lip of broken glass.

Most people abandoned this strip of land on the coast after the hurricane. Their white balconied shore estates smashed to toothpicks and twisted nails. Their strip of stores: barber shop, pharmacy, and funeral parlor; the part of town delicately called by locals as "downtown" was reduced to chipped chocolate bricks and panes of glass sprayed with grime. Their school house church was pulverized and blown away like powder to the merciless gusts. Now as the town remains abandoned, this man, our man on the pier, fashioned himself a hut from pieces of the wreckage. It is rather morbid, he ponders, to build a home from the shredded comforts of other people. Of good upstanding citizens who paid their taxes and loved their sons that never came home. But life still crawls around this sandy flatland. First, there are more fish in the sea. Perhaps this is the world without us, he muses.

He is not a man of bright tragic dignity. The other week he was kicking over boards of rotted wood to find a door knob he could wedge into the front of the hut. Under the weight of a permanently soaked armchair and a large cracked mirror, he saw what appeared to be a hatch in the ground. With closer inspection, he realized it was a portal into some underground chamber. A safe room. The man knotted his tan course fingers around the handled latch. After straining the chords of his arm, his feet wide apart over the entrance, the door opened. Sunlight glimmered in the flurrying dust, in a moment he had the sensation of casting his eyes into the mouth of a sea beast. The chamber was four feet deep and there was a purple mouthed yawn of a dead woman crouched in mud, holding an infant smothered with her apron. They used to sing these little ditties on the fiddle in the arm about women as pretty as she might have been.

In the damp evening of July, he felt a storm coming, the wound in his side stung its prediction. The sun never set and broke like a pink yoke on the horizon. Instead if stayed blind behind a looming cataract of cloud before the bruising black bulls of approaching storm appeared. Tonight, would be a bad one. The certainty of such impending violence prompted him to stoke a fire. Howling gales of mist and fistfuls of sand thrown into the air, pelting angrily upon the roof like marbles.

A scratching shimmied up and down his door, starting at the base like a demon trying to crawl under the crack of light. The man pulled his boots on and took a calming pull from a clay jug of moonshine. Then the door shook with a pounce of a creature.

He glazed into a stance, opened the door to permit a chute of rain to enter the hut. Before him sat a skinny black dog with one eye sewn shut. It's tongue darting in and out of its black nostril. Never before on this land had the man encountered another living creature with a personality. It shook off the rain and offered a low husky bark, peering around his pant leg as if admiring a familiar ghost behind him. Nodding in secret.

The man let the dog into the hut, closed the door in a slow sweep across the soiled floor. In light of the leaping fire, the dog shook its body in relief. The man placed his hand over the dog's soft flat head, running a thumb gently over the scrunched skin of its left eye hole. Muttering pity, he scooped a fish head out of the pot and waved it at the dog's snout before setting it on the ground.

Dawn, the man stepped out to inspect the damages. Shingles blew off into the seat and some rest on the sand far below. Despite the ferocious storm, damage was not as awful as expected. After observing the fates of his abandoned neighbors, he suspected this was a cursed land, bound to be destroyed again and again by the jealous angels. His shuffling boots woke the dog, who bounded to him and whimpered, setting a paw at his knee. It was difficult enough for him to feed himself. But maybe this brute could sniff out other animals to help in the coming winter. He wanted to believe in the minimal possibilities of such dreams, because he was lonely and respected another soul that could survive in these cruel isolated parts.

Walking the dunes with the dog, he set his stare upon the shoreline, its jagged fingered bluffs of rock wreathed in seaweed. Hissing clots of white foam clung to the beach, a rubbery dead jellyfish sleeping in its bubbly crest. He rubbed his knuckles on the dog's ears, lifting one and smirking at the pink black speckled canal. Ears are ugly things on all creatures, particularly humans, nothing but twisted flesh mounted on heads. He'd seen ears blown off in the war. He'd seen every part of men, tissues frayed by buckshot.

The dog barked toward the sea and then turned to land, skipping into the tall wiry grass in front of the smatter of a house. Its wood darkened by last night's storm. It resembled the twigs in a bird's nest. At this sight the dog began to whimper. The man knelt and embraced it, turning a cheek to its oily coat.

Collecting himself, the man arose and smiled into the single black bead of the dog's eye and a fear bloomed in his stomach. This place must've been the dog's home, he assumed. Inside the rubble of the past, the man came across a spectacle with the stem snapped off and two small stuffed dolls. The first doll was a black doll. The second was man. Several pins protruded from the back, he pricked his finger and drew it to his lips.

Dropping the doll, he withdrew from the house, and escalating anxiety made him aware of his breathing. He ran towards the hut, leaving the dog behind.

Miserable Son

I believe in transcendence. That in times of total chaos and complete tragedy, there is nothing more graceful and triumphant than handling the horror calm and noble. I believe the actual testament to man is his capacity to retain composure in the volcano, to have enough resources within himself to maintain balance. But what if this ultimate test of will, is not just a moment or an event? Not just a singular catastrophe, not just a reason. But a lifetime, an immovable element in who you are? What if you're the chaos and the resolutions are the scarcities?

Weekends are reclusive. None of the kids come near me since I'm the class creep. Reputation recovering in glacial measure since I stood on the tables in the cafeteria and professed my insanity. Spat on the flat ironed scalp of the girl I liked. Got caught spanking the monkey in physics. Got caught sharing chemicals in the locker room. Got caught in my profound spiritual squalor. Nobody wants to understand, they just want their little lives confined to their priorities. I'm outside the cage, outside the realm of relation. Remote and disobedient, I am relentless, penniless, and mercurial.

Friday, I come home and throw my bag on the table. Enter the den to see Mom sitting on the couch watching some soul sucking game show with a whistling theme rattling vulgar and synthesized. Commercial break she flips to divorce court and I'm fed up. Maybe I'll go to my room and sit on the bed staring out the window. Staring at the street and listening to a neighbor kid screaming *four, five, six.* Maybe I'll go to the basement and find that cardboard box preserving my Halloween mask collection. I bought a gorilla suit at a yard sale last month but it smells like vomit.

I like to steal road signs and I've filled my garage with them. My favorites are Dangerous Curves and Slippery When Wet. The laundry room has about fifteen baseball caps hanging on the wall. Each cap is sewn with patches of Super Mario, Joy Division, anarchic icons, pentagrams. Hermitage, I reside in this house all weekend and drink with mom. Told some people about it at school and they think it's the coolest thing ever. Mom and I sit on the couch, finish bottles and succumb to low budget exploitation flicks. Werewolf exhibitions and b/w b-movie sci-fi with Styrofoam picnic plates for saucers. She drinks with me all weekend because I have nobody else to hang with. When I'm upset we drink beers and watch war movies.

Never met my father, who disappeared one night at a bar. Mom says his contractor took him out. When I was a kid I liked pretending he was a secret agent on a confidential mission. I liked pretending he was shipwrecked and lived amongst a village tribe with a whole new clan of descendants. I liked pretending he never wanted to leave us. That he's really out there trying to come home.

It's amazing how good people are at repressing memories. Something special to be able to lock up feelings and shut out realities like unwanted children of your destiny. Chattering in feigned oblivion, focusing on the immediate aspects rather than your mistakes. You have to shun the pain because you can't change it you're only standing it. I cope with make-believe.

We were watching the Justice League on Saturday night. It was the episode where Aqua Man's baby is kidnapped. I wasn't listening to half of it because I was too drunk. Mom had her face goopy in some dermatological muck, halfway through it hardened into a whitish plaster around her cheeks. She looked like the grindhouse zombies we laughed at last night. I'm not good at holding my liquor like her. I drink to get drunk. She drinks to stay drunk.

During the credits my stomach was bulging. Unsettled, my jaws tingled and I jumped from the couch. Ran to the trash can in the kitchen pantry and threw up on the floor. Gray clumps of bread sticks and ziti pasta strew on the tile in regurgitated paste. Started to cry, my head hurt and my throat was chalky and acidic. Her orange slippers with the Dalmatian puppies on the toes nudged my hand. Looking up, I saw Mom frown. That same look I got for my report card. I curled into a ball with my knees inside my arms. Mom knelt down beside me and embraced me. I kissed her, running my sluggish tongue across her pearly enamels with specks of vomit.

We pretend it didn't happen and she hasn't hugged me since. Tried apologizing over breakfast but she just waved me off. She didn't want to hear about my confusion. It was my first kiss.

One evening on the weekend Mom and I sat watching the Twilight Zone. Gritty gray episodes with Rod Serling's lips curled around a filter less Lucky Strike. Tonight's episode was about a kittenish blonde who ventures into a nonexistent floor of a department store and realizes she's one of the mannequins that came to life for a month.

Mom went upstairs to grab her cigarettes and the doorbell rang. She told me to get it. Groaning, I scratched my ass and hid my bottle under the coffee table. Down the hall to the front door, a shadow dodged behind glass. Unlocked and opened, I leaned on the frame and poked my head out. A pudgy little man in a gray suit stood there, his broken nose healed badly between yellow eyes. He was the kind of man I could see right through. Solicitor at this time of night?

"You must be Kal?" the man offered an open hand. Shaking it, I turned an eye back to the house expecting Mom to appear.

"Yeh, how'd you know?"

"I'm your father"

I slammed the door and went to the base of the steps, hollering for Mom. She came down in a fleecy red and white striped robe with *Let it Snow* written on the pockets. Brushing past me and patting her black curls, opening the door.

"Aren't you gonna let me talk to my son?"

"Get off my property or I'll call the police"

The man studied the bristles in the doormat and peered over her shoulder into the hall.

"Please, I want him to know who his father is"

"You missed your chance" Mom confirmed, shutting the door and locking it. The man started beating his firsts on the door and yelling through the slashed net of the screen. Pacing the porch, shouting on the lawn, kicking over a gnome. We waited silently in the foyer until he left.

"You said Dad was dead. Who was that man?"

"He's your uncle"

"But he said he was my father"

"He is"

Mortified, I return to the couch and drink with Mom.

Bubble Gum Sailor

Sea tossed the vessel at night and Creighton slept drunk on the hat by his friends, Barfunk and Eliezer. Barfunk set out a deck of cards he swiped from a house in Lisbon, counting the jacks and queens with solemn contemplation, the black crescents under each nail tapping his grizzled chin. Creighton was asleep because his mind wandered in the night and visions of his young pregnant wife alone on the coast in a cabin with peekytoe crabs left him dull with regret. He had not been home in a year and she would have had the child by now. They had not seen land in eleven months.

In July, warm water brought sharks and Barfunk mounted the stern with a harpoon and shut an eye for aim. Creighton sat on a barrel of ale with his fingers stinking and mouth caked with salt. Eyes aged quickly watching mariners' slate with sweat roiling on the scaffold, eelgrass and seaweed floating on the gray water. Westward he pondered to the pregnant wife who did not permit herself to fantasize about his return, like he did.

Atlantic shoals imagined, he drank and stared ahead. Orphan, wearily confessing on the wooden eyed child of the sea, he thought about killing himself. Beast men around him rubbed their scaly palms, hungry for the flask of blood in a virgin. The yellow chalk of their saliva staining the rope. There was no hope in the desolate featureless plain of salt and brine unending in every direction.

Land was seen the following week. The beaches of an alien isle protruded through fog and Eliezer belched with glee. Lumbering towards the bow, the men waved to the fat flukes drained of blood, clinging to the timber and sobbing in thunder. A pouch of gnats hovered around Creighton's shoulders. Shore was seen. An arrow-eyed Aphrodite could be there, so could the loot of a Punic chamber, a greased worm or Trojan honeysuckle pyre.

Land. The men jumped the tide and splashed like dogs, barking happily and drunk, hugging each other laughing. The greenery was overwhelming.

Savage huts scattered the acre, ash pits smoked through vine. Women hooted at children circling dunes. The sailors frowned in skeptical hesitation, turning to the captain, stung with deception.

"Keep walking men. Take what you can"

Shell bracelets hung from the mens' fingers, feathered crowns placed on their scalps, rust medallions tucked in pockets. There was screaming, women pushing their children towards the wilderness. Barfunk emerged from a hut looking for Creighton, shoving past villagers.

Creighton was vomiting in the sand, gagging on ale. His shoulders were seized and he was brought into a hut, dark and damp with incense and simmering drums.

"She's a psychic, Creighton. She knows English. She knows how my father died. Ask her anything, she can't lie"

"Do I have to pay her anything?" Creighton slurred, his head rolling around on his shoulders, never opening an eyed.

"Just ask her something"

"But what if I don't want to know anything"

"She's waiting."

The old soothsayer grimaced as she polished the tortoise shell, humming and angling the shell so rainbow prisms glinted in the dome scraped of flesh. Her yellowed eyes watched Creighton's tongue, lapping at the salt on his sweaty wrist. Creighton lowered his chin to his chest and stared mournful and skeptical, shutting his right eye and clearing his throat.

"What's the name of my newborn child on land?" Creighton asked, rubbing his jaw with the back of his hand. Snow was in Creighton's mind. New England snow, ice capped and clean. No tribal oracles.

"Your child has no name. Mother and child dead" The soothsayer spoke, curling her bottom lip into her leathery jowls, wagging a feather across her neck.

Creighton left the hut. Sat in the sand and said nothing. He considered his wife, her skin, her ankles, her fingernails, her anger, her globe of joy, her wedding dress, her child from thumbnail to mammal in the unseen waters within. Holidays alone, she must have sat in their bed and scorned his departure countless times. She must have sold her jewels to sustain the household. She must have suffered before leaving.

Bring loss and luxury, bring castles and courtyards, bring empty pastures of sea.

Fascist Vagina

Stuck in this dungeon. Gone dim with hunger. The basement is pockmarked cement with fluorescent bulbs screwed between ceiling pipes like arteries. This is the incarceration tank I've been sealed inside for five years. Maybe five years. Cell mates include a nuclear physicist named Cyclone Stevens and a young girl I've nicknamed Candystripe after she got her period three years ago. Candystripe brushed frizzy orange bangs out of obsidian eyes that turn jelly black when she cries. Cyclone Stevens is the husband of the woman we call Fascist Vagina, a female dictator that overran the earth with nuclear chaos that led to our imprisonment. To spare us. To torture us. Candystripe is her younger sister and I was her closest colleague that helped her defeat the UN.

Fascist Vagina thirty-four and the last time I saw her was a week before I came here. I was trying to flee the country and three armed guards knocked on my door. It was in the middle of packing, bolting from closet to suitcases as fists beat against my door like hollowing stone. Ran to the bathroom, opened the window and got my ass out halfway before being pulled back in on the yellow tiles and beaten. Woke up in this basement with my forehead split in a river of blood. Woke up with my hands in cuffs and my clothes swapped for a dusty beige robe. Woke up sobbing because I knew Fascist Vagina won and she would always win. She would always be lurking in my shadow.

I executed all operations from the oppressor. Took orders, filed names with snipes, passed off missile coordinates and orchestrated Fascist Vagina's oligarchy; starting from aggressive bureaucrat to volatile insurgent. Cyclone Stevens recalled a miscarriage with his wife. They said she was a woman prone to her emotions and she was not silent about her grief. The public loved her for this. Fascist Vagina is the most charming, articulate, magnetic and determined person to be thrust in front of a camera. Policies consisted of uncompromising domination and totalitarian workshop. Unsettled every president and prime minister. Labeled a Hitler with ovaries, Stalin on estrogen malfunction. The United States was the central nemesis, forbidding her tender inclination towards warfare. Laughing, both amused and admiring, she slipped a nation into the vaporous helmet of radioactive ash. This world belongs to one woman and she is unstoppable.

Once a day, three loaves of bread and a jug of wine. Once a day, Fascist Vagina blurts the calendar on the intercom. Once a day I bash my scalp on the walls before guards stop me and stick my ass with needles. Cyclones Stevens and I have beards to our navels, biblical patriarchs stinking and sorrowed by our descent into madness. Our robes are black with feces and hands trembling in uncertain purgatory.

Over, again, more of the same remorse I funnel into my windowless chamber. Can't remember the way rain feels on my face and glasses, sunlight warming shoulders. Can't remember her voices but I still see her birthmarks, vivid and flawed. Can't remember the last time I smiled awake hypnotized by a simple peace. I didn't stop Fascist Vagina, I enjoyed the luxury. Reservations to every bathhouse and bistro, seven cars and a pool. Butlers. Drivers. Secretaries. Ceremonies. Billionaire revival. Pockets steeped as I sent sons to battlefronts and lent my face to periodicals.

My children were ashamed of me before my captivity and fled the country with my wife. Left me to my mansion as an empty lawless tropic of loneliness. Kept myself efficient and channeled my rage into my profession. Cyclone Stevens and I take turns expressing our outrage on Candystripe. Her sisterly resemblance to Fascist Vagina inflamed us. Her vulnerability makes her a target.

Sometimes we beat her and start screaming at our expired dreams. Screaming with spittle trembling on our chins. She is a bystander and is in a greater feud against myself. She's a distraction, a momentary relief before returning to the reality that I will die in this dungeon after her. We were men who once had everything and now breathe in bronchial shallowness.

Cyclone Stevens and I became good friends. He told me about his marriage and I told him about mine. He doesn't know that I am here because I slept with his wife and that miscarriage she had was mine. I was partially responsible for her neurotic fall out. For that vacant cellar in his heart, filled with questions unanswered and starved like our narrow torsos.

I have not permitted myself to remember happy moments before the imprisonment. They are not a life I can accept anymore. I reason Fascist Vagina keeps us here, her husband, her lover, and her sister, to protect us from the outside that wishes to destroy us. We're her disciples, her corrosive cogs in confidential captivity. We are a liability. Knowledge has made us impermanent but substantial foes.

Candystripe heaves hysterical in the corner and if I'm feeling particularly tolerant I embrace her. I will embrace her and whisper in her hair that she is a gift from god and I'm sorry this happened. I will whisper that I'm a coward like Fascist Vagina. I will whisper sad hyperboles drenched in selfishness. I will whisper an oath to fight, a declaration to survive, despite the increasing evidence that we will never live outside this cage crusted in vice.

Look around my hole lit with the filament of prior dreams, scrawling out any sign of an empathetic deity. My imagination errs on the side of vengeance. Burning alive pedestrians with nuclear catastrophe. I was a merchant of murder, clairvoyant war monger. Farewell to any coping mechanisms, strategies for sane survival. Sweating, I stand here listening to the walls.

Strike me down. I'm an involuntary patient of Fascist Vagina. I'm lucid with dreams of flight. Since society has been withheld from me, I've formed a population of my own that have conversational tea parties in my head. Speaking back and forth, it's a tennis match of soliloquies forged between bloodshot eyes. Glassy pupils contain the world outside, never seen but longed for. My lover recoiled on me like a child's tantrum, lingering in my sinewy limbs like poison.

It was the eve of the sixth year in the dungeon. Cyclone Stevens masturbated in the corner eight times a day. I took my habitual plunge on Candystripe but she started muttering nonsense to herself too. We are all going madder than before. Madder than the violent disbelief that plagued the first two years. Madder than our faintest ideas of madness.

Loudest voice told me to do it. This voice was the friendliest of them all, the softest and effeminate. This voice calmed me when I lay awake in black perilous night, soothed those tingling impulses to kill myself. This voice was my favorite and knew me best and cheered my daily courtship with disaster. The voice said the girl had to die.

It said that if the girl died, Fascist Vagina would surrender. Candystripe was the only sibling and salvation in the veins of our Lady Death. To kill would kill time. We would get out. We could live again among the people and disappear. The sister was the last link to the dictator and the remaining heir to her queendom.

Did it at night as Cyclone Stevens slept. Did it while the lights flickered and diffused a senseless guilt on the door. Did it at the quietest, most cruelly inanimate event of the day, the mating ritual. Hands found their way around the neck and gripped tighter. Tighter. Hold. Tight. It's something special to be the remaining prospect of civilization in a basement. It's something to sneer and snide at the concept of hope. It's vain to hope, all I rely on is revenge. I watched myself like God as I did it. Shaking my head at myself. Not in anger, but shaking my head like when a puppy shits the rug.

Morning guards came in and threw me against the wall with Cyclone Stevens. Fascist Vagina came on the loudspeaker, clearing her voice you could hear her exhale from a cigar.

"That's it boys" Words clipped and candid. Cyclone looked at me, confused and betrayed.

The squad was three men wearing gas masks. Cyclones went first. Blood contained the only intense color I knew in six years. Adrenaline fed-awe, I grew hungry watching.

I gawked at the guns and pictured Fascist's Vagina's teeth snapping a cyanide capsule. A new nation would inherit our reputation and a new generation would speak our names with regretful bluntness.

Graceful, I lifted my hands to my head. Addressed the transient parlor of my mortality. Ached no more, distressed no longer. I didn't have to stick around for the defeat. Nobody will ever care for me. I like to think all fates are predetermined and that helps with the guilt. I like pretending this was out of my hands and I operated according to the chronological necessity of my era. Looking up, the sky is blue in both hands. Looking up, I'm not here.

The Vicious Spirit Avenges

77°4N 70°38W. In the seaside ice town, located in the hutting blue at the brim of an arctic tundra, W. Lamb conducted a most ambitious investigation. The Inghuit settlement of Hiurapaluk. Population of sixty-eight. One side of the village is shadowed by cliffs while the other half bares the flat bone colored shores into the water. Lamb spent the past several months translating Inuktun with a history scholar that studied the area with him. Both men were researching a supernatural rumor within the polar region, a most alluring atrocity, a sea witch.

Qicha. She that can possess all forms and climb onto your fishing boat while you sleep. Queen of driftwood and eelgrass, in a natural state is said to open her foul dead lips with her purple coral tongue snatching the cold air on her shell teeth. Lamb is unaware that his reputation as an outsider seeking forbidden information has worn through the small population to reach a certain group. A cult of fishermen's wives who worship Qicha, have noticed W. Lamb. Amaruq, he is named by them a wolf of speculative design. As to punish the unwanted stranger, the fishermen's wives have conjured Qicha and earned her presence on land for only one day by having each member deliver the witch a fingernail from each of their children.

She has been summoned. The ruffled back of her scaly cloak has followed her invisible tracks on shore, to answer the nightmares of her people. Biting gusts, promising her village women the soul of the insolent scholar. With his gristles of esoteric empowerment, slant muscles, and properly vapid intonations.

Pouring her howls all over the cold night, a ghost recalling a deb to the past. A gangrene goddess craving the human soul. Perhaps why, it may be asked, could the appetites of a mythic wench suffice to a dull human, a vessel of odor and flatulence? Because humans have hidden from the monsters sentenced inside the sea ice, far from their humans and their beloved nostalgia for living. These grim entities that live in the ice, despise their lively descendants, forgiven through death from the infinite loneliness Qicha must withstand.

W. Lamb's research relied on phantom folklore. His meager satisfaction was derived from analyzing the tales that horrified the people that communicated it. Qicha was not a sea witch of vast and encroaching power but a popular figment, a bedtime warning. To W. Lamb, Qicha was a preserved artifact of human irrationality.

W. Lamb rested in his tent at the base of the mountain with his colleague in the neighboring shanty, snoring under the seal skin cloak his accommodating matron provided. Fierce winds, a mighty storm in the ocean, showers of hail and dead fish were approaching the unlucky quarter of the archipelago.

Kanungayok tonrar akkisartorpok. *The vicious spirit avenges.* W. Lamb awoke with an intense back ache. His discomfort was hushed by the whine of cold wind searching the village.

"Walter?" A gentle entreaty startled the darkness. W. Lamb sat up.

"Who's there?"

"Look at me" The man came closer. W. Lam lit his small lamp and held it by his ear, registering the features. Lowering the lamp to his notepad, he felt the anxiety cramping his sides.

"James. Come here. Let me touch you. You don't know how much I've missed you" W. Lamb's words drew the entity closer. James glittered in the haze of the lamp, warm black billiard eyes that clawed at something in W. Lamb, something from a nether sphere he avoided the past four years. James knelt to Walter's wrists limply displayed on the cot, his thistly black moustache shelving his upper lip that kissed and worshipped each individual finger on Walter's hand. James nibbled each knuckle the way he had on those solitary balmy summer evenings at the university. An embrace in a messy fourth floor office that ended in a holiday of papers tossed to the floor in the torrent of unwelcome desire. Back when James was still his pupil.

"I still love you," James admitted. This was not like the confession that contained the shame that drove him to the straight razor that December.

"Me too" Walter confirmed to James, a boy who while alive, feared his father's eventual knowledge of his son's elicit passions. A son that chose a coffin afterward.

The acclaimed anthropologist W. Lamb subsided and left only the Walter who loved beautiful broken things.

Walter shut his eyes, because like all mysteries he could not perceive with his spectacles, his eyes did not deserve them. Walter wilted under his hot breath, relief under the lone demonstration of affection he permitted himself in years. Froze his greatest desires in the northernmost barren tundra, bloomed forth a curious erection.

James' skin grew course and cold. His kiss revealed the cracked shards of bone in his mouth used to shred skin. Qicha's eyes beamed while she kissed W. Lamb. He shoved her away, and felt her body disperse into a thousand flakes of ash. W. Lamb dragged his body out of his tent into the snow, where he lay until morning to be retrieved by the fishermen's wives.

Animal Man's Apocalypse

He lived in the mansion on Phantom Hill as long as I could remember. My friends and I used to play baseball in the yard. At the time I was a devoted member of the Barnaby Gag. Driving around in Mickey Ayatollah's minivan with a baseball bat wagging out a passenger window at mailboxes. Arrested twice. Once at 15 with state troopers and once at 16 for being drunk, local pigs. Sundays we played baseball in Animal Man's yard.

You had to climb over the stone wall to get in. The expanse before the porch taunted our peripheries as boys while we crossed the street and managed a peek through the black steel gates. Animal Man's property was a joke. Some said the place was left to the church, I like thinking so. The front yard was burnt yellow grass and plumes of angelic dust. Paint on the front door faded white like dirty cartilage. Slabs of firewood on the portico never used but scattered on the muddy floorboards. A broken rocking chair in the corner under brass wind chimes.

Sunday after St. Patrick's Day, we were all hung over but Mickey Ayatollah insisted on the baseball tradition. We did it because we loved Mickey even though in the car ride we all had a turn taking the slightest opportunity to start a fight. Our throbbing eyes squinted from the daylight as the radio flipped on. I was sickest because the night before I got Claudia Carpenter drunk so she'd let me fuck her. This time when I went over the stone wall I vomited on the way down. I didn't want to play baseball, I wanted to fist fight. An hour after the game started I got pissed at Mickey, mocking Claudia Carpenter. Mid-pitch, I swung around and threw the baseball into the second story window of Animal Man's house.

What the fuck man. Fuck this shit. The voices shot around. Nobody was happy with what I'd done but I had to stand my ground like a man and back myself. I told Mickey Ayatollah he could suck cocks in hell. All my friends started walking away from the game, heading to the stone wall. Put my hands on my head and turned my back, let them leave. Overheard Mickey telling the guys what a shitty friend I was. Claudia Carpenter, look what you cause.

Alone, I sat on the porch and watched them disappear. Handled it like I didn't care, scoffed, stared away, but stung. Stung by my own stubbornness. Got quiet, heard the engine of the minivan hiccup over rocks. Gone. Crouching near a barred window I sat for some time. Time used to study shredded cuticles, spitting on the step and looking over my shoulder. Smoked against the door before sticking my freckled nose in the window. Could've sworn I saw an animal prowling between the sofas. Pressed my ear on the glass and heard a faint squawking.

Stepped to the front floor grimacing at the lion door knocker. The front of the door splintered with ivy. Leaned the right shoulder of my leather jacket into the door until it opened. Dust kicked up like powder in a long rectangle of daylight. Shit. That was the stench my hung-over nostrils combated. Looked through blind shadows to perceive mounds of feces rotting holes in the floorboards. Growling shape lunged forward from the fireplace. A tiger emerged and got to the door before I did. That only left me the house to room.

Tore across the marble foyer, I could hear the chandelier shaking with the commotion. Hiked up the steps, ran to the closest door, sealed tight. Banged my first for admission. Door swung open and I realized I was inside what I wanted all along.

Animal Man your face was not leathery with time. Your hair wasn't long and gray to the waist. Your eyes were not glassy blind gray. Your hands did not tremble on a staff, were not wizard-like hands with moles, scars, nails doubled in length, yellow. You were not naked and slick with blood and berating me in a burlap robe. Animal Man you were only maybe fifteen years older than me. Two years less than my brother Jimmy in Hoboken. Your hair was shoulder length, blacker than your eyes. Your beard were ringlets that clung to your neck. Your eyes were not wrinkly but glistening coals in smooth pale stone.

"What are you doing inside my house?"

"I threw a ball in your window. I wanted to know what it looked like inside. I thought you were dead"

"Well I'm not" Animal Man groaned, stroking his beard with a bony alabaster hand. My eyes fell to his bare feet on the carpet, a pile of shit several inches away.

"What's with all the shit?" I asked, shrugging with my hands in my jacket, pressing loose dimes into my palm.

"I have many pets. You wanna see?"

"Sure, just keep that tiger away from me"

"You haven't seen anything" Animal Man entered the hallway, strutting down the magenta carpet whistling. Paintings on the walls of fluffy fat old white people in ermine and tuxedos. I felt their frozen expressions melt with disdain as they watched Animal Man escort me past the bathroom. Cockatoos. Toucans. Parrots. Eagles occupied the bathroom, checkered teal tiles splattered white and wet black feathers clinging to the toilet bowl. The translucent pink curtain slashed. Chrome bathtub knobs crusty yellow and caked with shit. Mirror covered with scratches like glaring through fog.

Monkey straddling the grand piano and a koala leaning imperially into a leather armchair, cobra slithering through gold handles of a mahogany desk. Two sheep sat on the floor near the radiator, blood staining wool and a wet mass emerging from its legs.

Downstairs, Animal Man threw a deer leg at the tiger to distract it from my nervousness. We shuffled onto the back patio to the pool. Algae clumping along the surface and broken by the snout of a sniffing alligator. Tool shed home to rabbit. Garage to wolves. Basement to Bonnie the gorilla.

Proud of his exhibition, Animal Man concluded the tour by leading me up the steps back into the room I met him. Closing the door behind me, he closed his eyes and sighed, straightening his posture and coat hooks. I sat on the mattress, a particular spring insistent on my right butt cheek. The obtrusive odor of feces was forgotten when my eyes glued themselves to Animal Man's bitten bottom lip.

I've shown you my kingdom yet I don't know your name"

"Lobotomy. I renamed myself when I ran away"

"What are you running from?"

"Regret" I answered, leaning into the headboard of the bed. Silence ensued and I distracted myself with the dingy lavender curtains on the window. I put my hand on my zipper, "Ten or twenty?"

"Ten or twenty?" Animal Man repeated, confused.

"So probably ten" I said, pulling down my zipper. Animal Man swatted his hand and turned away.

"That's not what I meant" he admitted, paused, and then resumed, "I have something I wanna let you in on." He muttered, shifting his posture on the mattress beside me, shaking the fishbowl on the dresser. Dying a trillion deaths of humiliation, I lowered my hand before glancing idly on Animal Man's precarious glare. Those eyes interrogated my lanky posture, curled in spontaneous shame.

"I have some important news." Convincing me by kneading his knuckles and apologizing for his enthusiasm, "Today's the end of the world"

I cackled with glee. Sifting my chestnut bangs between fingers the laugh started harmless in my collar before it spread out of my face into the room like a poison gas, indifferent amusement.

"Stop laughing or I'll feed you to my tiger" Animal Man blurted, clenching the mattress and white flames bursting in his knuckles. He hopped up and turned on the television, taking a couple seconds for the gray picture to harden into clear images. The dim apparition of a newscaster announced, *a Meteor is headed to earth of extreme proportion and unusual speed, further undetected until this morning, our technology is not prepared for this. The dow...*

Face drained, I thought about my future stolen from me while I was playing baseball with my friends. I was just a teenager, pissed off. And now it's over.

"I've been predicting this for years!" Animal Man announced, pleased with himself. Confirming this and throwing his head back with his eyes to the ceiling, taut neck blanketed with his thoughtful palm. Should I have congratulated him? Should I have believed him? Should I have told my father I was sorry and told my sister I didn't mean to touch her that way in grade school?

"I need your help" Animal Man professed, desperate. Animal Man explained that he was collecting all the animals like Noah from the first testament, his mansion was his ship. Very close to shrieking, I sat opened up with confusion on the mattress like a careless autopsy. I assigned words to Animal Man I used to think were cool and flatter myself with, like psychopath.

The mansion shook and the windows began to shake, flaming cysts raining from the sky. Glass blew out of a window pane.

"Quick, open the doors and windows. Animals be free!"

"I thought we needed them?"

"Did I fucking stutter?"

Stormed the room, shielding my eyes to the plutonium peroxide haze through the window, burning comets devouring the globe in radioactive space, falling out of stars born to hate us. Tear it down, let the world whiter in my blood shot epileptic eyes twitching down the halls. Doors swung open, windows lifted, waving my arms at the zoo Christ, twinkling with phosphorescent feces splashed down furniture, streaking walls and seeping floorboards searching for escape, preliminary motivation.

I did it for him. I needed something to latch myself onto and bury my alienation deep in, reach a summit of my worthlessness. I was manic, pulsing adrenaline run dry on the animals stampeding to the doors. Animals free!

Nothing ended. Just got real burned up. Animal Man sprung from the roof. We survived, his animals flocked the streets and pecked, mauled, stalked pedestrians, vehicles, developments, daycares. Animal Man was dead in a flight from life, suicide during an apocalypse is a coincidental misdemeanor.

Thorpe in Pieces

Lost his hand three years ago in Fallujah. Thorpe was infantry, cargo strapped to his shoulders and the steel pins clacking against the rifle to his chest. He recalled that day many times, lying on a gurney, sleeping to the groans and shuffling of sneakers on linoleum. Bed pans and IVS, first month before rehab home in Omaha.

When it happened, he was deaf for a minute, opened his eyes to see the bloody stump of his hand with the bones sticking out like a snapped off toothpick. His hand five feet away, a mangled black lump with palm open to sky. The smoking wad of a nearby car, gas stirring rainbows in the merciless sun. When Thorpe lifted his head to check his body, someone slapped their palm to his forehead, keeping him flat.

In the hospital they got cards from kids in grade school back home. Crayon on construction paper with bubble letters, shouting pride and good wishes. Thorpe collected a dozen and then kicked them all to the floor. The papers on tile trembled in the air conditioning.

Omaha, he lived with his sister, Clarice, and five-year-old daughter Tammy.

Tammy was afraid of him when he first arrived. He was the first person she could stare at in her life, yet alone close to her, that was missing a limb. It frightened her at first, like he was a bit off Gingerbread man. She stared at the prosthetic he rested on his napkin at breakfast. She didn't speak to him, shuttered at his embrace and clung to her mother's pant leg.

Thorpe couldn't get a job when he came home. He made people uncomfortable, except maybe a couple older men who felt heroic if they asked him about his service. Otherwise nobody wanted to see him, see what was happening in that other place, somewhere else. Keep it in the TV set. They wanted their lives in liquor stores and gas stations buying cigarettes, there wasn't a war here. No crisis wanted.

One afternoon Clarice needed Thorpe to watch Tammy while she attended a PTO meeting. He decided to take Tammy to the local park, get some air and maybe some gin. Government sent checks, and the rehab facility was a slow drive at dawn. At the park, Tammy sat on a bench with a strawberry ice cream cone.

"How'd you lose your hand"

"A dragon" He muttered, kicking a rock across the trail. Tammy ignored this and ran over to the playground. Thorpe followed, watching.

"C'mon, build a sand castle with me" Darting to the sandbox, she began to release streams from her fists onto her bare legs. Thorpe sat beside her and became anxious, the sand made him think of Iraq as Tammy filled a purple bucket and patted it.

"Why aren't you helping me?" she asked.

He said nothing and could smell the sweat on him again, seeping in rings under his armpits as the blonde hair on his arms winked in the sun. Tammy got sand in her eyes and started to cry, so Thorpe carried her to the water fountain and leaned on the lever.

She lifted her head out of the chrome dish and shook her wet tendril, drops scatter on the cement. He hocked back saliva and coughed before placing a hand on her shoulder and returning to the minivan in the gravel parking lot.

"I want more ice cream"

"You just had ice cream. You'll ruin your dinner"

"No, I won't.

"I said no"

Tammy unbuckled her seat belt and threw a tantrum, kicking the back of his seat with her rhinestone sandals, smacking the window. The tears dripped from her ear lobes.

"Dammit I said no. Sit down and put on your seat belt or I'll pull over"

Tammy didn't listen. She climbed over the arm rest between them into the front seat, banging her first on the dashboard. Writhing and shrieking, she scratched his chest, grabbed his prosthetic arm and yanked with both hands.

He pulled over. Not moving. Not breathing.

A police cruiser parked behind them. A cop came to the window.

"What's the problem, sir?" the cop asked, his glasses shifted down his face as he spoke to expose purple prints on each side of the nose.

"Nothing. My niece is throwing a fit and my hand came off"

"Do you need help"

"No, I'm fine thank you"

"You okay to drive"

"Yes, officer, I am okay to drive"

The cop returned to his car and Thorpe shut his eyes, listening for the engine to hum away.

"I'm gonna tell mommy the police were here"

Frog Messiah

Come back from war and drag yourself through hell for this. Come back from war with eyes sewn crooked and demons of its own regiment. Return home, that place you kept sacred unscathed from chaos. Voyage through bloody crematoriums with your gun to your chest like a patriot's crucifix. Atrocities of the mind manifested in myriad corpses and the war is not over. Cities left charred desolate.

Wake up in the afternoon to a sky skimmed of color. Haven't seen the sun in three years since the exhaust blinding the atmosphere. When it rains you have to take shelter or drops will burn through your clothes. Sometimes the night's stay longer than the day and its blackness, none to separate. Dawn. Never get enough sleep. I used to dream about home. My wife and son. Won't see them again.

Entered a forest midmorning. If you call it forest. Burnt armless pillars, sinking in yellow clay. Stones burgundy and the outline of a mountain a mile away, bluish temple in meridian fog. Every other hour I have to stop walking because the coughing builds up, brown phlegm. The air is killing me.

Bugs grew ten times in size after the war. Insects you could once see and smirk at with a newspaper expanded to mutant ratios. Houseflies and bees became poisonous because the air gave them too much, congested with toxic blood streams. Animals like the household dog, cat, or goldfish have been gone for years. Vegetables returned to their wild ancestral state. If you step in the ocean your flesh will slide off your bone in radioactive foam. Most rivers the same, creeks, brooks less so.

Seasons lost varying degrees of heat, cold. It's always November. I'd like to think a rescue will come, some savior to flutter down from clouds.

My fear is that every passing hour is a flame dwindling into the soot, my meaningless life. Living apart of a plateau singed and featureless, sick for the past. Sick for the past like there's a hole in me that can't close, bleeding over and again. Whimper, pity yourself with the pain all over and nerves inside out. On your skin, everything is too much.

Keep head up, eyes forward. Continue. Nothing can stay. I'm crying out with it. It won't last, it won't last. I won't last. Raging my pale armor of skin through unmoving earth, still as glass, nothing to grow out of it.

Cave appeared. Saw it while walking. Doorway into a damp air misty, deaf and dreary darkness. The opening was draped with black lava stalactites, soil shining with yesterday's rain. Steam rose between granite stones.

Croaking, it was like a soft purr. Croaking. I heard its insides mesh together when it swallowed. Threw my bag over my shoulder, hooking my finger on my trigger. I ran out of ammunition years ago. It's just for show.

Found a book of matches at a gas station I stumbled into last month and kept in my pocket. Matches saved for nighttime check for poisonous bugs. It irritated me to use them. But this was something special, it had to be. Struck the flame and held the thumbnail torch. Walls were naked, bereft of color and warmth. Walls were the same color as the orphanage I saw in the last town. I cried in that orphanage, all those little plastic chairs turned over and some finger paint scraps hanging from a clothesline. A chalked letter on a board, poised in mid-arc. Their scorched wood chip playground.

"Come here" a voice said. The match burned my cuticle. Damn. I lit another. Didn't see anyone. Nobody inside this cave.

"Down here. Down here" Resounding him a humble fondness near my ankles, I stared down and shuffled my boots. There was a frog between my toes. I knelt to the dust with my match to see. Thumbs clenching the match, numbing in disbelief. This frog was speaking to me.

"I've been trying to get your attention. You have to listen to me" The frog spoke, its voice low and paternal, urging me. I'm just crouching there looking inside myself with pure dread. Sat down in the gritty trench and wipe my eyes with my forearm. Tears were coming out, actual tears at my own misfortune.

"Are you listening to me? This is important!" The frog barked, leaping onto my thigh with a violet striped good sinking into my pants, stinging. Stood up, screamed, rushing my palms down my body to reassure myself of its completeness. My face went in my hands and stayed there a while, shoulders shook, heaving nauseously. Sucked the saliva through my overbite, straightened my spine for confrontation. It's just a frog, a harmless amphibian with a vocabulary. It's just a frog. No bullets or bombs. No knives or native loyalty. No allegiances or ammunition.

"Please, I need your help" It rumbled and cleared its throat. I tried to be casual as my nose registered the stench of bile secreted between its slick legs. Why would I be this frog's dire reliance, why would it need me to grant patience to its rattling please? Yoke of puss between jaws slapping in language. I listened.

"I am the second coming of Jesus" the frog declared, "I am the son of god and you will take me to the people"

"There are no people. Just some survivors like myself"

"They must hear my judgement" It asserted, plainly unforgiving. Relentless, the frog saddled my leg, crawled to my stomach, stuck to my shirt, decided.

"Why did you take the form of a frog?"

"Does being a human feel good right now?"

"I thought you were used to not feeling good"

The frog laughed. Should I have been grateful and mystified by this cameo? Should I have relinquished fully to my knees and begged for guidance? Should I listen when voices beyond my own direct my destination without the slightest regard for my independence? I gave in to my elusive messiah, like many men in the eyes of God crusading for paradise, gave in my fear, not of death but the pain of life. Gave in to the frog and agreed to chauffeur him on my shoulder to his shy barren prospect of civilization.

Left the cave and ventured through prickly atomic cross brow of ruined trees and plains. Grassland now wasteland, crusting over and perishing in the breeze, hot slivers of passing molten air, festering in lungs, pandering to whims of decay.

Out of the cave. I was nervous with questions for the frog clinging to the mantle of my shoulder.

"I will bite you with poison if you fail this mission" The frog muttered, hanging close to my skin with its mouth open.

"I thought you were forgiving?"

"Forgiveness was burned out of this planet" It answered, measuring the vacant fields, daylight marbling the hills, sifting through the polluted miasma. We came to a creek with water reduced to neon powder. I could hear the acid eating the ground.

"What are you doing? Why have you stopped?" The frog asked, panicking, blurting its thoughts. I looked to the sky and perplexed the watery cataract before wrapping my fingers around the frog. My nails piercing the jelly membrane of its body, spilling wine down my chest.

"Stop! Mankind will be damned!"

"It's already damned"

"Don't do this for your god!"

I threw the body into the sizzling creek before me. My isolation was familiar and predictable, unlike this frog. Isolation that does not reconcile for the greater good. Isolation that grieves for a garden. Isolation that made me demand questions without answers. All we are is what is left. All we are is what is here, and what is here is stripped and unwilling to repent.

Steady is the hand drained of love. Steady is the hand drained of longing to change. Steady is the hand that refuses closure.

If I had taken that frog to the people and told them to worship it, I'd be strung up. Like him. Like a veal. Now we're both ghosts.

Shot Glass Ashtray

Casagna, thirty-one and a child again! A child who cannot go anywhere without permission or chaperon. She has a red eyed ankle bracelet the judge put on her a month ago. The court settled on house arrest and now she can't leave the home she shares with her husband, Obrin. Legal fees and public disdain made her a monster the teenagers joked about on the bus and parents cringed at. Couldn't go to the grocery store or the pharmacy without being scolded. After teaching sophomore English at Central for six years, her employment was terminated when her lanky student lover mentioned her corkscrew fellatio to his friends. Called into administration, confronted, dismissed, arrested.

The lover was fifteen, an exchange student from Cote D'Ivoire named Serge. He was living with a fellow classmate who delivered her name to his parents. Casgna, blind from her hemorrhage of light and ether, admitted to her husband across from the plastic folding table, her cuffs cold against her inner thighs, that he wasn't enough for her. But he stayed. Obrin always stayed.

Relatives started flying in to take Casagna's hand and pin her to the living room couch and encourage her to seek help. Obrin went through a period of silence around her for some weeks. This amused Casagna because he was a professor in speech pathology. On Tuesday and Friday nights, Obrin sang and played guitar in the corner street coffee shop for a heavy-eyed audience that failed to yawn. His students were his only fans.

Obrin became immune to Casagna's momentary costumes of sincerity: the hand on his sleeve as they watched a movie. The article marble of that fever hand cut his knees like scalpels, and he glared livid like a wolf with dials for eyes. Optic spires of his stare, a dull needle that wept for a lost garden. The smile she projected with lingering expiration of her past kindnesses. She was his duplicitous dumpling. Obrin rationalized her infidelity with Serge (inflated by the boy's age) as an existential excursion. He wanted it to be seen by his friends as some sexual compulsion of entitlement and rebellion to the inherent formalities of the institution. The subject was not forgiven but neglected. This was the expendable generosity of his understanding.

The aperture of her desolate eyes was scorned in an attic of irregular fucks and the potent crystals of despair. This tearful plain of exile. To Obrin, Casagna became the silhouette of a Euphrates gypsy with a tracking device clasped to her bare ankle. Wild hair. Aspiring to falsities, that Serge really loved her, the blushing sorcery of lust. Throwing herself down to the floor like a frothing convert to the ultrasonic dormitory of her insane neediness. He understood but could not tame the beast in her dungeon. A deformity of passion that was not soothed by any manifold traffic of his words.

Her shouts tore through his scalp like a kamikaze squadron. Their home was an infected sea swimming with infantile urgency, libidinal alienation. Her advances were abortive. He'd wilt in her hand as she glazed a dull observation on his flaccid extension like a vegetable in the supermarket. Casagna succumbed to a phobia of stairs and lived on the first-floor couch with portable fan and radio blotting orgies of pop music. A body curled under a blanket on the sofa in embryonic parody.

The phobia of the stairs was a recent development in Casagna's tidings. The antagonizing beige carpeted shelving that toppled each other up into the second floor held the greatest weapon of all. The fear was so intense and committed that the mere sight of the stairs plunging her into fits. Obrin hung a blanket in front of the living room that spared the slightest edge of the bottom step from view.

In the second month of her house arrest, Casagna's fear of stairs was given a sibling, a phobia of windows. The gaping glass rectangles contained the bright forbidden anxieties of the outside world. They knew the snow, rain, wind, sun, every single day and any moment could shatter from the weight of this time. A bird could fly through. A branch could break through. A bug could crawl through. A snake could fly through. A man could climb through. Someone could watch through. Every window was a waiting opportunity for danger, to enter and never escape. All rooms on the first floor had windows in them except the bathroom and basement. She moved to the bathroom. She did not change her clothes or bathe. She only left the lavatory if Obrin was at work, to snatch a bag of chips from the shelf in the hall.

Casagna's days were smeared in a fog of disabling convictions about every specimen and spectator she allowed herself in the humming fluorescent tile and fruit patterned wallpaper. The sink was ringed in an ivory crust. The white porcelain toilet a bitter citrine stained black. Anemic and hostile. When Obrin tried to pull her out of the bathroom, he clenched her wrists and attempted to extract her from a corner behind the toilet. His exorcism cut short with a kick in the crotch and slammed the door.

Obrin, once calm, combed, caring, compassionate professor of speech pathology, turned bearded, unpleasant, unsleeping. Over the span of five weeks, three students complained about his treatment to the chair. Obrin was warned that one more complaint would result in probation.

The casino welcomed Obrin despite the grueling harshness of his wife's illness, or the disapproving moral repugnance of the university, or any institution, any business, any preliterate thieves. And the world was too much. But in the casino, it was always air conditioned. You were greeted. You could drink.

I need you, every winking light sang out to him. Blue metal barstools and beer sinking in your organs as your eyes fill up with bravery. In love again! Obrin in love again! I do to Madame Casino.

The hours Obrin spent on campus teaching were reduced and he never came home, instead renting a room in a neighboring hotel and gambling the night until he was too drunk. Woke up the next day, hobbled into a lecture hall and sat in silence the first fifteen minutes of class. The students were uncomfortable, maybe this was an experiment they reasoned. Some picked up their bags and left. Laughing with their friends, louder and louder. And he sat there.

Scabs clustered on Casagna's arms, scratching herself again.

He felt young and daring in the casino. He was a necessary aspect of the casino's survival. Obrin's goal was to move forward, stake enough to gain enough, start a new life. The solution was self-erasure, eliminate yourself from the situation.

New Year's Eve, Obrin saddled up and played the worst hand of his life. Lost everything, all the money he withdrew from his account. Mortgage, car payment, insurance, electric. *You can't do that!* As the chips were scooped away. His voice grew louder, he was no longer sitting. And then he was outside, holding his shot glass and smoking. Tapping the ash inside. No more to be filled. Once the joy, the whiskey inside. Now only the cremated remains.

He drove home and sat on the porch an hour before going in. Opening the door Obrin inventoried the furniture and lamps with a disconnected curiosity. Mice skittered under the kitchen table and a large frosty spider web laced the foyer's clock. Down the hall with a dozen empty cereal boxes lining the wall. A tv remote facedown on the carpet, batteries missing.

Casagna opened her eyes and laughed when Obrin entered the bathroom. Her chilling descent into laughter shook him as he knelt to her and took her in his arms for the first time in months. He held her close, as she continued to laugh into his green jacket, the zipper printing a jagged worm down her face.

Ocean Encounter

My name is Jupiter Keez and I am nineteen. I dropped out of college last semester because I don't know what I want out of life. Came home to my parents, Rupert and Violet Keez. My mother, Violet Keez, kept yelling at the dog as I tried to tell her in a plaid cushion beside her, that I was getting out of the university and coming back home to understand my place in the world. My father, Rupert Keez, is a famous magician who came after the holidays to drink in the other room.

Violet Keez, with her lemony eye shadow and chin frosted in gray springs of hair. Her breath biscuity and manner gone taciturn in the cohabitation of marriage. Mother coerced me in a game of chess as a distraction. She didn't like the news of my dropping out. I figured she was secretly panicked. Maybe I was disappointed a fight didn't happen, some dispute I could finalize in a slammed door. I didn't know what I wanted her to tell me, but this wasn't enough.

Rupert Keez, just came home from his most successful tour. He was gushing glee like a child at the dinner table the night before about Tangiers and Barcelona. *They loved me!* He said and we did not blink. Father made us sit around the computer and watch videos of his show. We laughed at the punch lines and jeering jocularity. My father's magic show is a two-man team, my father and his partner, Kurt Blossom.

Kurt Blossom is a close friend of my father's and I've known him my entire life. Funerals. Weddings. Birthday parties. A constant figure. As a gift to us for his success, my father claimed he booked a round trip to Mexico for our two families. Keez and Blossom.

Kurt Blossom brought his wife, Ura, and his three-year-old daughter, Yolandi. Ura's the whitest person I've ever seen. She's sixteen years younger than Kurt and my mother doesn't like him for this. Ura was always kind to me. When I was sick with mono in middle school she baked me burnt tuna casseroles.

My older brother, Roald Keez, married last year. I called him about Mexico and he was more excited than me. He scolded my lack of enthusiasm but he scolds anything I do anyway.

Mexico was alive. A truck bounding down the street with six amplifiers advertising the local beer that resembled the light watery urine you have after drinking it. Sea the same color as sky and broiling under sun, a lattice of sunlight bending around like white wires on the seafloor. From the land, a shelf of dark blue water could be discerned, sea grass and a ten-foot drop. To the south, a slim wedge of land jutted into the sky, rocks pocked and chipped with the fade of salt. A man with one leg selling seashells asked a woman to dance. A couple sat in their chairs under the shade of a palm tree next to a stray dog with flies hovering over its ears. Buildings pink, orange, purple leered down in their trill gaiety. There were protests the day before, a thousand marchers with microphones calling the government a mother fucker and the thrill wailing of a portable siren in someone's breast pocket.

I decided to go into the water. Ura was rubbing sunscreen on Yolandi, who couldn't stand still. Dad was sleeping under the umbrella with his hat over his face and hands folded on his chest like Cleopatra. I smelled the cigarette smoke of the teenagers in front of us.

Sprung my towel and hopped down hot sand, through the umbrellas cropped up between reclining chairs and plastic pails. My feet burned as I slipped into the water, splashing wet sand and foam jumping up my knees.

The water does not curl into waves here, but glides back and forth. Diving under my hair spread around me like an urchin. Kurt Blossom stood beside me with his hair washed over his head shiny and metallic. He bent to the water and submerged his elbow in the surf. I felt his arms dip into me in an amorous shock. I could taste the acrid sea salt glistening on his back.

"Hey Jupiter, enjoying the water?" Kurt asked me, an eye clenched to the sun peaking above me. My insides leaped, imbibed on a single stare. Eyes that had no specific coloring of amiable intrigue.

"Yeah. It's something" I muttered, slowly crawing closer, the venomous contraction of this desire making me dizzy.

When I was a little girl I performed in my father's magic show. I would cramp myself in a box and plunge through a trapdoor. Pull a bouquet out of my eyes and shout at pigeons flocking from my skirt. Kurt Blossom would throw me on his back and run down the aisles of the theater. I did not speak to Kurt. Did not speak as I descried a glimpse of Kurt's pubic hair when a wave slid his bathing trunks down. Intuitive and unapologetic, I knew that I had racked myself with forbidden anxiety in his collarbone long before I recognized it.

I pulled myself from the waters and lumbered back to my towel, that vapor of disillusion swamping my thoughts. Ura wore big sunglasses that made her head look small. Mom was raving about the conditions of the restroom. And I found myself yearning. Chiseling at my confusion, I consulted my senses for rebuttal. Senses overwhelmed and blunted by my loneliness. I don't mind being a backburner.

Kurt Blossom approached us, slouching in the sand and glaring in the heat. He shook the water from his hair like a dog and again, I was drawn without reason. I watched him pick up a towel and retrieve a beer from Mom's straw bag. Watched him bounce from item to item, compelled, entranced, mortified with absolute oblivion to my studying gaze.

Had difficulty extrapolating my irises from the decisive limbs of Kurt. Felt stupefied and anesthetized by the aloof posture of Kurt. Painted on terrific platitudes. Ideas of mesmerizing intimacy. I gorged myself.

Riveted and banal, I hugged my knees to my chest and watched children bolt to the current. Fever of the quietest despair, I grew disturbed. Ura buried Yolandi in the sand. I felt like a splinter. Making this family portrait perverse. I felt like a crack in the mirror, the bleached stone, the stain in the mattress. Anticipating.

Shish Kabob Sex Organs

So, I've this new role I just auditioned for that's gonna make me a bigger star than I already am. My agent called me three hours ago and said I got the part and I could not be more thrilled. It's a script that has more daring and originality than anything I've seen before. The characters are beyond comprehension, immensities of complexity. Nobody out there is doing stuff like this.

The movie is called *Shish Kabob Sex Organs* and it's about the death of suburbia, crisis in the middle class, sex, drugs, mutilation. The central character is a thirty-nine-year-old husband named Otis Irving, who will be my sonata of gloomy anguish. He is an associate director at a prestigious legal office in his suburb. His two children attend a private school and his wife is a crabby caffeine addict that exercises all day. Otis Irving is breaking under the pressure from his exhausting family, the animal climb in the office, kneeling before a deity of tedium.

My role will be to capture every monotonous claustrophobic shift into madness in Otis Irving's life. The role offers a great payout but I agreed to work for less just to have the part. My girlfriend left me this morning. She claims this role is consuming me. I guess some people accept the truth and others shut it out.

Shooting starts very soon. Otis is the most intriguing man I've encountered in my life. This director is a visionary. I saw his first film a long time ago in my college years, when I was acting in this teenage sitcom called *Two Brothers with Guns*. I met my wife on the show when she was nineteen, she played my younger sister. She introduced me to my current agent who has taken me from stardom to monumental success.

Back to my story. I was talking about this new film I'm starring in! This plot just has to be divulged, I can't help myself. So *Shish Kabob Sex Organs* was originally supposed to be a slasher flick but then my director decided to give it more multitudes of meaning and Otis Irving was born. Anyway, the guy is fed up with his wife. One day he meets this jailbait girl outside a bookstore on his lunch break. They have an immediate attraction and tease each other. He tells her she's too young to be smoking and she tells him he's too old to be flirting with her. Of course, he loves that.

Otis Irving goes into the store and has some coffee and broods over some pulp bestseller, crinkling the binding when his agitated eyes catch sight of the jailbait girl approaching him. She sits with him and makes an awkward moment more awkward when she admits she's a sex worker and sneaks him a proposal. He is shocked, flattered, and a little appalled at how young she is. He looks at her and he just can't look away. He needs her or that image of her or whatever. But he can't hold back, he has to say yes! He can't disobey his deepest wishes when he is so repressed and solitary! She knows this. She senses his need and serves it.

At this point in the story, Otis Irving is battling his morals and all perspectives on life he's gained in almost five decades on earth. He's got a thousand images of the world he's known in his mind. Here a little of cinema my director is gonna flash before his audience's eyes:

Styrofoam housewives clutched in the squeaking spray tanned hands of materials. Ill-mannered moguls of corporate behemoth getting sucked in stalls and bars. Empress of the Thai palace with the purple rug that weeps with the smell of sardines. Dim darlings bending a bruised knee under neon hallucinations. A child pulling the trigger of a water pistol on a yawning hound. A priest muttering saints to a flat hand shifting east to west over an empty grave. Infants consoled with cocaine and cigarettes. Men in minivans stroking babysitters getting fucking in the ass by salvation. Politicians barking prophecies with a finger swelling towards supermarket motherland with cervical polyps and pop ditty stereos.

You get the picture.

Shish Kabob Sex Organs is going to be the film people remember me by. It's going to be the next smash. Otis Irving's withdrawal from sanity will be the next chapter in the way we tell stories. Now I have to keep going with this.

Otis takes the girl to his house while his kids are at after school specials and his wife is at palates. She comments about the interior design in a snide jealous way. He ignores this because he doesn't understand this.

In the bedroom he snorts cocaine off her toes. Then he choked her too hard while they were fucking.

Her body goes to the basement and ten minutes later he hears the garage go up, his wife and children are home.

His wife is unpacking groceries on the counter. Delightful father bonding ensues before dinner time: Otis playing Thomas the Tank Engine, Otis reading a popup book. Not a trace of evil is sensed by anyone.

Okay, I need to pause and explain my filmography for the past five years that has prepared me for a role like this. I starred in a made-for-TV biopic about serial killer Gary Ridgeway. I guest starred in four episodes of an HBO show called *Man with a Dark*

Side, about a psychotic ice cream truck driver who is the perfect balance of righteous and ruined. I co-starred in a drama called *Terrible Lust*, about a high school softball coach who abuses his wife and has a nervous breakdown. It can be said that considering my resume, I am the best candidate for Otis Irving. The director is letting me prove myself.

People told me I changed after my son died. The worst was right after, I was drinking too much. But I found something inside myself that made me keep going and that is the universal lie of art. I returned to my roots of creation and distracted myself from the tragedy. There are sides of me I can't open up again or I would lose myself and cry. But the days are new, there are opportunities sprouting everywhere and I can't let myself falter.

One of the reasons I like *Shish Kabob Sex Organs* is because it's adventurous, it's not afraid to be disgusting or misunderstood. Nowadays it's in not to fit in, but then rogue vanities like violence are a sign of unique empowerment. The evil is more candid and complicated. Those we admire are useless without evil.

Otis Irving may do awful things but I feel for him, I relate to his displeasure and composure in the throes of a distressing marriage and busy lifestyle. I connect with his debilitating nausea for the banal. He's just a man who craves meaning. He's just a man who chases his vitality. He's just a man who's not afraid to lose everything.

Otis puts his children to sleep and his wife knits in bed. He enters the garage, drags the girl's body to the basement, rams a fire poker up her vagina. Her wife discovers him, calls the police. A colleague in his law office defends him, spares him lethal injection. Spends the rest of his life in a hospital for the criminally insane.

The first time I read the script I was hysterical with questions. I had to find the soonest time to audition. I talked to psychologists about the cycle of mania and psychopathy. Even interviewed a couple men about what they felt when they crushed someone's trachea. Some people claim movies like this make hurting women look fun, but people get upset over anything anyway so it doesn't matter.

A woman is standing in the doorway with a clipboard. She is wearing glasses. She taps on the door with a pen. I say nothing, she has interrupted my train of thought, she's interfering with my meditative reflection.

"Mr. Irving, time to take your meds"

Charon in the Discotheque

I walked under the purple stains of trees. In the darkness no one found me. Just the way I like. Slipped into the train like a poisonous fog with my head bowed to my boots. When the ticket man sweated down the aisle through my car I turned to the window and watched the world flow out of me, I saw nothing but the orange hexagon of a streetlamp every fifty feet. Everyone in the car was absorbed in a secret unto me I didn't deserve to know. Periodic jolts after a reeling break, stop after stop under a fluorescent dinge I thought about how if someone came onto this train with a gun, a mass shooting phenomenon, common place now, we would all be frozen shut and dead like sardines in this tin can tunneling through darkness.

I'm going downtown to get fucked up at a club. Yes, I want sugar. Right now, my unbreakable paramours are horse tranquilizers but I try to think everything in life is a phase.

The False Hope started out as a bar with shrimp take-out and under glamorous new management it evolved into a discotheque. Tonight, I'm coming here in my rave disguise, furry ankle muffs and glow stick bracelets. Last time I was here I dressed as my mother, adorned in the mute ugliness of her flat pointed white shoes and purple sweater with gold buttons. Then I defiled her image by fucking a junkie. It's relatively easy to give up on yourself, just adopt the persona of someone else. I've spent most of my life pretending to be other people and nobody knew it. I practiced the art of disappearing without moving and used my good cheer as a form of self-preservation.

I entered the disco with the faintest twinge of gloom in my hands as I swept a tear from the corner of my eyes. I've come to weep easily as I've gotten older. I could be on the bus watching the streets leafed with garbage sit still in the sun, a fast food paper bag crunched up and hovering over a subway grate, the book store with the vinyl awning proclaiming WE SHIP TO PRISONS, or blind past the Precious Angels Asian American Rehabilitation Center, bilingual neon shuttering in the dark. An urge climbs into me to cry, over the super sensitive hypocrisy of my gratitude for every stupid detail I like in the path of. Every click of silent deprivation, interrupted speech or shifting stares around me, draws me nearer into the welling circumstances of my depression. Therapists, friendly but remote, weaving through the smog of my confusion. We pay to be told we're okay, we're doing all we can. If only I believed myself.

In my office during lunch break, a freshly indoctrinated graduate posed us questions about gendered body language as all the women talked about their inexplicable compulsion to cross their legs, to hide their hidden hairy vaginas. I noticed that people love to talk about the inane pointless habits they groom themselves to obey. *I like to cross my legs at the ankles. I like to play with my hair. I like to apply chapstick.* Every second spent distinguishing ourselves. To believe we're all weird, nobody is like us and we are all uniquely trapped in our childhoods.

Tonight, I can't take the heat of those strobe lights choreographed to the drag sway and percussive humming. It feels good to be a part of something, a part of a force larger than yourself in a crowd where everyone surrenders to the loose epileptic freefall of their limbs. Some imitate coitus while others spiral alone in the center. I see friends laughing together, pulling their stringy arms toward the dance floor, laughing hermetically about their feigned embarrassment but their eyes secretly lit with the torch of release. We eliminate our pasts and replace them with the claustrophobic incoming now. The inescapable, unaccountable now.

Blinking in the mirror of the ladies room, the sweat clinging to my skin cold I have to coax myself out of this sudden fear I am dying. Something's not right. I am misshaped. Regrouping on the floor of the stall, deep Dalai Lama breathing, I exit the bathroom, flinging my demons to the corners.

On Friday, the kids are out, confident in their IDs, girlfriends laughing on barstools in miniskirts high waisted and cheap.

But it comes, without permission. It rushed over me in an icy hunger for closeness, my dead boyfriend standing in the middle of the dance floor. Why is it I always return to him? In the recesses of my loneliness, his face floats upward from the depths. To reassure me I will never heal.

Everyone is dancing around him, their hair catching the lights like dandelions. Lightly attached to my nightmare. His posture is not rigor mortis tall, but bent and he's looking at me. Those eyes, wide and loving like a child, feel me, know I'm vulnerable. I like to believe there is a language of forbidden love, an eternity pressed between two arms lightly grazing each other, the heat of a body collapsing and unfolding and emerging from a lair inside. Souls mingling, dim euphemisms and poetic trash about helpless infatuation.

"C'mere. It's our song" he nods. This lets me pardon myself, pardon my imperfections and the subtle earthquake in my stomach that flutters into a cold snow drift. An invitation to the underworld.

"I've seen what you've been through," he says. These immediate words disengage me. I have been caught by him. Consoled, and I reject it. Leaving the club, I head home with the vague secondary prize of solitude.

Eater of Children

Was it not the sun that crowned you, as we lay alone, imperial and untouchable, side by side? And now I'm without you. A wordless sacrifice I shared with a crate of rotting oranges in an alley covered with snow, recalling your memory. My long white teeth denote a manifest dullness. Muttering alone in the dripping cabled tunnels of a subway. Inside earth like a worm before the angelic astronautic ascension two stories above. By a window, my hands on the glass like a child. I've told you this story many times. Don't make me do it again. I'm going to the forest, where the eater of children is said to live. Once I join her, the uniform reliability of all my hopes will die.

Snow, antiseptic white, its eyes closed on leaves. I feel myself gazing through a strip of parted curtains, my fears and ignorance framing the landscape. A brown creek glossed in ice nearby. My hostile enclave of demons grinning between the shrubs. With me I bring a rogue child from the city. He is five, he had nobody to protect him. His knuckles grayly thickened from the cold, his blonde eyelashes starchy with fallen snow. I promised him a fire and a turkey dinner with my wife and three children at our cabin.

"How much longer?"

"Not much longer" My hand hovering over his cotton sweater, the color of crusty mustard. Together we walked, my past and his future toddling side by side in disturbing adversity. The boy pulled his collar over his nose as the wind blistered his lips and powdered drifts of snow. Danger's lucid stride leading me, it's fawning parasite, deeper into its thicket. The paranormal silence awarded by snow, each particular crunch of footstep a punctuation; leading to the end of this little boy's short, simple, forgotten sentence.

At first, indiscernible in its fog, no snow lay around the cabin. It remained untouched by weather, blind from sun or storm, preserved in ancient apprehension. Its mask of mist and rotting odor, forbid my entry, which compelled me. Abrasive black pine walls with an aperture carved out by urgent hands, formed the hole by which the eater of children, my hostess, observed us. The door parted with a cane of bone in her hands, fingers gnarled around the silver handle like pale roots. She came forward like a marble hunchback, obscure ailments and dim opal eyes, speculating our presence.

"I bear gifts" I said, looking down at the boy in my nervous fatigue, my procured premium trying to shake my grip.

"Come in"

I pushed the boy in front of me and kicked him in the pants to get moving. The door locked behind me. The Eater glided, in footless ease, to a crow with crooked white eyes that scanned her visitors like a disapproving spouse. The crow perched on the mantle of a fireplace of enormous proportion. We were led to a table clumped with the waxy fat of burned children. The Eater's chair had cushions sewn from the clothes of her guests as she turned the cane in her hand, a charming scepter given her by a screaming nine-year-old girl. She sat before us motioning to the chairs on the opposite end, a very large chair and a much smaller one, reserved for the arrival of monstrous couples. My cannibal shrew sighed, depositing eyebrow hairs and fingernails in her pipe, and smoked with discreet pleasure before speaking.

"You bring me such a delightful boy. What is your request"

"I want someone back from the dead. Completely restored"

The little boy jumped from his seat and ran to the window where he punched his fist through, gasping and frantic. He seemed to have forgotten. This is the darkness. There is no other ending.

Up from my seat, I strolled over him as he tried clearing the glass, but sobbed as a diamond shaped shard the size of his palm stood from the back of his wrist. I slapped him down and he cried for his mother, a mother of needles and naught, sleeping in a river of little boy tears, thirty-seven miles away.

"It's your turn" I told him. The Eater arose and crouched to the child, sprawled on the floor, covering his eyes with his blood hand. She stroked his hair and hummed, I was revolted by this unexpected affection. Soon the boy stood, clutching his hand and sucking back the flood of tears, the breaths spaced into devastated hiccups.

"There is a wash basin near the rocking chair, my boy" she said. He walked to it, past the enormous fireplace, always burning but leaving not a single ash. In the basic the water blushed with blood and I grew impatient.

"Are we doing this or not?"

"It's not so simple. I must teach you the agony of longing to expose to you the meaning of true passion"

"This is a game. I didn't come here for a game" I said. I picked the boy from his chair and removed the large shard of glass from his wrist, held it to his neck, and demanded to hurry the transaction.

The Eater paused, becoming sullen.

"Walk into the fireplace," she said. I glanced at the leaping flames and put the boy down. The heat licked the buttons of my shirt, they spoke to me and I drew closer, preparing to dance.

I walked into the fire. Nobody was there. Not even me.

Midnight Show

Cupcake Dallas worked at the Martini Olive. Sugarcube is what Sir Donahue called her to the fans, his voice thick and dark like oil spilling into the storm sewer. Ice cubes clinking against the microphone, his third J&B of the evening. Sir Donahue always had his share of blow before the show, and if Cupcake stayed past lights out when all the drunks spilled the last of their blood in the bathroom sink, Sir Donahue would unearth a deck of cards from beneath the floorboards and strip to his bow tie and suspenders.

The lovely lewd Cupcake Dallas had gelled black arcs for eyebrows that rose and fell with her drunkenness. Hair was curly lavender locks that looked gray in the darkness. Angel wings inked on her spine, wings made of wood and ice.

An amethyst shimmer of a navel gem. Black bikini with a detachable leather snake that wraps around her waist and slides between the cleft of her ass as she dances. She wears white heels with spikes on the back and rainbow-colored guns patterned on the toes. A filly pink lace garter she sewed herself in the clumsy damp flat overlooking a factory lot.

Last year she let a seventeen-year-old boy who slunk into the club take photos of her. He said he was a photographer and he was fascinated with all aspects of life, especially the gritty darkness. Cupcake agreed, flattered and lifted with a sense of significance to this small mistaken artist. The boy took the photos and never came back.

At the Martini Olive you get your varieties. From beetles in sports coats and trousers to the ripped slung denim and corn rows. You get the monkeys from out of their universities and tasting the world one bill at a time. The occasional elderly ogre who knows what he wants and tells you so. Some ask Cupcake about herself. She can be anyone she wants. *I'm Cupcake Dallas from Dallas. Chicago. Cleveland. Nashville. Salt Lake City. Philadelphia. I'm twenty-eight. Twenty-seven. Twenty-six.*

Sir Donahue is the emcee and owner of the Martin Olive. He has a rusty mane he combs from his left eye. An eyebrow piercing and chest hair peeking from the top button of his collared shirt at the base of his throat. Three tattooed knuckles on the right-hand spell SIR. He has this casually charming and virile shadow of a beard. Has a criminal record of petty thefts and arson. Has the Martini Olive, once a joint owned establishment between Sir Donahue and a partner. The missing partner.

Cupcake Dallas came out of the Kitty Lounge after doing a line with Neptune and Venus, Cambodian twins with matching candy cane nipple tassels, clapping their hands in cheer for Cupcake. DJ Damnation turned on the smoke machine and the room ached with howls of laughter without faces and dubstep thumping in heels of silver stilettos, strutting down the stage and twisting her torso around the carousel of golden pole. DJ Damnation had a wooly auburn beard and a shaved head. On his naked scalp was a blotchy frowning verdigris stain from when his step brother threw acid on him. One eye blue, the other brown. He's the man who hears everything and says nothing.

The Cambodian Twins, Neptune and Venus, are foiling farces of each other. Venus is playful, Neptune is pensive. Venus, the younger, prettier twin and more talkative. Older twin Neptune, sullen and pouting.

The Martini Olive is Cupcake Dallas' home. Sir Donahue is father, keeping her fed in place. Neptune and Venus sisters, revering Cupcake as queen of the club with the love in her eyes and bills in her garters. Mary of the midnight show, holy rosary sucked between the blooming peaches of her breasts. Tire iron tears crying in the soul, gunmetal eyeshadow like two burned holes in a sheet. Cupcake Dallas, keep spinning around that pole.

Keep those eyes shut and lick those lips. Keep your head above the sea. Forget the baby powder you once had on your elbows. Forget the sterile sponge of gurney, rolling into the elevator like a cloud on wheels. The world has no time for crazies and loners, so stop trying. Life is full of disappointments, so stop trying. Love is transient and fate is stronger, so stop trying. Or else all those hyenas in their liver spotted jowls will cast their chains upon you, and Sir Donahue won't like that.

Cupcake Dallas, stay cheap. Skin broken in burns of illegitimate touch, forced dialogue, laughing in filled space of her own insidious debates with dignity. Cupcake Dallas takes Sir Donahue better than the twins.

He'll never know the great passion she's capable of, the great ivory phoenix of passion with its inebriated seraphim. One time a drunk stubbed a cigarette in Cupcake's shoe. One-time Cupcake saw Sir Donahue and DJ Damnation shove a duffle bag six feet long into a trunk. One-time Cupcake had a husband and son, but they're as close as the ears to the toes, and their lives lived elsewhere. Cupcake Dallas, just pretend from eleven to two: you're a star that shines in the dim circuit of time, loop the rope twice before you fall through.

Stone Eye

Old Stone Eye cast sleepy poison on the sun. Stone Eye felt the window off tides, a shuttered gasp and Stone Eye never trembles. Stone Eye stares forward with all the lovers printed in his eyes. Stone Eye's dusk is the fallen gaze from his alabaster brow, crushed to sooty darkness. Stone Eye with tulips in your pores, why do I ask something from you? Isn't your existence enough?

Stone Eye woke up one morning and had no mouth or nose. They had flattered into his face and were oily mounds on his chin and between his cheeks. Features melted into his face while sleeping. To this day he defies science or explanation. They said they fed him through a syringe in his arm. Very little was understood of his condition except pity and repulsion. Stone Eye glared back from his faceless vessel to muffle desperate grunts that scared the children and animals. His aqua chrome irises sat motionless in his skull, unspoken animosity in his resignation. You could see that weight on Stone Eye from the way he carried his shoulder when he walked. You could see an irate speechless anatomical malfunction, punished without articulation and stunned deaf to his own voice. Stone Eye, could we have been friends?

Our town was petrified. Barbecue-picnic-office, his name pulled into conversation to poll interest. Uncle Byron said he knew you in the fields and that you were like any other man. Any other man, nobody special, a face in the crowd. It's strange to think how you can be near someone every day before tragedy swoops down and pulverizes them unsuspectingly. Stone Eye you were any other man to my Uncle and I'm any other man to everyone else.

I saw you once before you disappeared, Stone Eye. The pond before you disappeared, Stone Eye. The pong on the outskirts of town, summer evening and all the kids went home for dinner. Climbing the drooping willow that leaned over the water, I shimmied up the trunk and skinned my knee twice on the bark. I was trying to make it to the higher branches to untie the tire swing over the pond the kids used. The kids trashed the pond, banana colored wrappers floating on algae, a used condom in mud and soda cans flattened.

Grimacing at the garbage and the youthful audacity I envied, I would teach the kids a lesson.

Stuck my arm out until it hurt. My longest finger only graced the rope, a knot that seemed a part of the branch. Knees cradled the trunk and sneakers tightened around my feet in sweat. Almost fell. Stung my palms meaty from bark, clinging to the tree like what Kafka, my pit bull, used to do to Dad's leg. Looked over my shoulder briefly and the shape jostled through the tall grass. It maneuvered through logs and stumps, sweeping its shadow along moss like the exhale of a ghost. You wore a sewage green ski hat over your face with two holes. I had to get higher up the tree or I would have collapsed.

Stone Eye, you were the broken warrior alone and unremarkable. Watched you step to the pond and kick off your boots, dirty bare feet with calloused toes dipping in the water, chalky and calm. Stood at the banks and lifted your hands to your scalp like removing a crown. Scuzzy wool drawn from your face. Your head looked like a balled-up piece of clay. The space where I imagined your mouth would be was just a divot in your skin, thin and translucent with purple veins spreading to your neck. Nose was a lump in the center of your face, decorated in scabs.

Crouching, Stone Eye ran his thumb back and forth through the water. Feelings muddled in his face, lowered eyes scorched from the sun, shaking in his own reflection. Hands entered the water and stayed there for some time. Wrists jerking in grayish fluid as a sopping bracelet slid up his sleeve. Cupped hands brought water to his face, slapping into his forehead and dribbling down his cheeks onto his shirt.

I was drawn with the same vulgar curiosity someone feels at a traveling carnival. That curiosity and decaying allure in monstrosities always burned me out and stranded me in sorrow. Stone Eye, this town treated you awful and you didn't leave for the longest time. Were you afraid of the unknown more than our town? When you left I was proud of you. You'll never know my admiration but maybe it gave you strength when you didn't know it.

Broke a branch in the tree and Stone Eye flipped his blind features on the willow. Cursing in a bashful whisper with my face imprinted by bark. I waited a minute and looked from my spot to see if he was still gouging the willow with that speculative frustration. Stone Eye saw my face peering from a shroud of leaves and stared mute. Sat there and watched me until I hid my gaze. Looked up two minutes later and you were still there studying me. I was afraid you would climb up the tree after me. I was afraid you would shove me in the pond or hurt me. I was afraid of a still and quiet stranger.

Got up. Stone Eye raised himself from the banks and crammed his feet back in his shoes. Turned away from the pond and followed his path. Jumping down from the willow, I stumbled toward the pond and invited his retreating back. You did not hear me Stone Eye, and you travel on, mightier than the earth that reviled you. Mightier than the fist that ground your identity out of flesh and the shrill screams you could never utter.

Those eyes still watch me. Ten years later and they watch me with tears from the pond. They watch me like there's no honorable reason for anything. Why does that stare linger behind my eyes? Are you somewhere in the ground staring up through dirt? Am I seen as clearly as I once was, determined with a swift observation before tossed to wind, judged?

Stone Eye, I am your only witness. Stone Eye, I am your only audience. Stone Eye, I am only your voyeur. I am a bystander. I am a refugee like you, a hyper sensitive recording device. I am lost. I am mesmerized. I am you.

Take it anywhere you want, passing specter, Stone Eye. Ingenious anonymous, Stone Eye. Miraculous misery, Stone Eye. Lightning strike, Stone Eye. Final foe, Stone Eye. Far away I am someone else. Any other man. My someone else.

Destruction Enamored

Standing in front of the mirror, Truman Morrissey slipped his fingers through the chrome loops of the scissors and hacked away at his hair. Clumps of black fell around his feet, dead ends spiraling to the tangerine carpet. The mirror spat out a gangly self-employed photographer with a gift for the quiescent posture of a hobo glittering in pain, a prostitute asleep in a doorway with her eyes caked in velvety magenta eye shadow, a giggling child with their toes cast on pavement studded with rain. Truman Morrissey was not unusual in his capacity to relate to alienated figures of society. These discarded veterans brought him pleasure, their wide eyes tingling with jaded abandon.

His lens captured the cold creations of a deity whose passive resentment reverberated through volumes written by old men in dusty rooms. The warts and deformities held more intrigue than the glazed membrane of dismal common. Bleeding out the separation from the dream to the retreat from the dream, Truman Morrissey hacked away at his hair. *Cut it off!* Spoke his woe of clarity.

Drinking himself stubborn, clad in leather vests stuck with pins of peace signs and subtle remarks about marijuana. Aching for original flagrance and beating out the inspiration with a pipe of panic stripped of love. Reasons for meltdown in the bathroom would insult the complexity of the entire situation. After the hospital people asked him, "Why did you want to kill yourself". A question he could not stand.

Disability checks now, affording his disorder a tax break and clinical validation. Filing out the door, one by one, the medics scratched their receding hairlines and washed the blood from their wedding bands.

Banana Alamo, a mother of three, attended his AA meetings in the local Presbyterian church. The AA meetings were casual, sitting in a circle, sipping curdled tea. *Do you drink because you're angry?*

February blizzard brought Truman Morrissey closer to Banana Alamo. Undressing beneath the sheets, Truman and Banana forgot her marriage, his feast and famine art career, their crude lifestyle and intricate quirks of overbite and facial scars. The trysts sustained through winter, bathroom stalls, bulletin boards, scheduled coital interrogation.

He placed his hands on her blonde scalp, bleached strands sifted through fingers. Brown eyes under mascara shelves compelled a contagious fire in his loins as his mouth pursed frothy with longing. Muscles tightening in desperate transactions of glances and caresses. Her timorous smile, cracking across peach strips of skin called lips, a silky glade along her back. Melted and sunk under sheets in embrace, clinging.

Cradling his asphodel and hyacinth of pleasure that spilled out his ears and onto the sheet, his head throbbing with incredible affection, and he knew then as she lay on the bed with lust coagulating in her cheeky parlance, melodic, he could never live alone again.

"Move in with me"

"No, I have kids" Banana muttered, reaching for her white leather purse on the floor by her suede ankle boots. Withdrawing a cigarette, she sat up against the headboard. Tumbling halos of smoke drifted over the mattress. She left the bed and draped a satin kimono over her naked body and shuffled to the television across the room, flipping it on and throwing the remote on the bed.

"The blizzard is expected to stay in the area another twelve hours. We recommend you stay inside and avoid roads which have iced over. Forty-six inches of snow expected. In case of emergency please call your local...."

Images of roads covered in thick layers of snow appeared. Mailboxes capped in white and highways foggy and desolate. Boxy letters in the corner offer the temperature and time. The news anchor adjusted his tie and stared into the camera at Truman Morrissey and Banana Alamo in envy.

Channel flipped to a game show with a host slipping flirtatious remarks to a beauty queen in pecan tan with a grin she wielded on the crowd like a sword of glittering dental profanity, patting a manicured hand on a letter cube. The wheel spun and the colors clacked with possibility.

"I told my husband the roads were too dangerous to come home, that I was staying at a hotel" Banana garbled while chewing her cuticles and stifling a sigh.

Silence ensued, awkwardness placing itself between their bodies. Truman was at unease picturing her children. He'd seen wallet snapshots Banana shyly offered in her car. It made him sick to imagine her husband. Sitting perpendicular at a dinner table with ravioli and biscuits between them. Banana was graceful in her resentment, she could stick her hands to her sides and smile by her husband at parties. Brave and revitalized by a dirty sore fuck in a hotel.

Two days later. Afternoon Fed-Ex stopped by to deliver a package to Truman. He thanked the driver and placed the box on the kitchen table, wrapped in translucent red. Retrieving scissors from the drawer, he slit open the package. Stunned, he threw the box against the wall and two amputated toes with purple nail polish shot in opposite directions across the floor.

He picked up the scissors and entered the bathroom door. Cut hair clumped in the sink where the medics rinsed their wedding bands.

You or No One

When I was seventeen, I learned the magic of saying 'hello-how are you' to people. People love to talk of themselves, seeking any vague small opportunity to exploit their greatest trivial charms and woes. An avenue straight to the heart. If you listen with each minute to minute, acre upon acre is gained entry into their soul. As of your soul, an entity composed of only individual thoughts, the benumbed and weary listener, it molds and mounts into a lonely statue. Awaiting their questions. Inquisitions and persecutions. Desires and furies. Wait like the angry tempest gathering wind, unanswered.

I will never be free of you. But you are free of me. You have not seen me but I have seen you. I hear your face within my heart like a great noise that I will never conquer. I have let you conquer me. Yet you do not know, you walk about life with this prosaic tedium of your failed and provoked passions, unaware that nearby yet so far, like a ghost on the other side of the mist, I beckon your name in my sleep. And I damn myself, over and again. Your beautiful, wretched and powerful name tears me apart to a whisper, in the lonesome quarters of my room. This lonesome quarter where ghosts and humans mingle unaware of their mortal tragedies incurred. You have the medicine of my soul, the arsenic to my heart beat. I know what is best for me, and I follow it dutifully, vainly and martyr-like, distempered and hating myself the whole pathway. I bow. I pray. I sacrifice these petty days to my life to the secret altar of your fantasy.

When I met you, my mind was a place of peace and neglect, which with time, had overgrown in grass and weeds. You tore it up with vehement disregard, for you have never known my love for you. Let us speak of you, the suggestive and detrimental, you.

You announced to our colleagues that day your wife was pregnant. I, who had been nursing my forbidden longing for close to a year at that time, took this as a betrayal. Then you reached out into my darkness, with your special hairy hand, extended in the criminal air, waiting for the sharp exhale of an axe.

We were alone in the dark room. I stood, bent and submissive to my shame, over a tray of finish. Watching the developer gleam alive fragments of my picture until its entire exposed landscape blinding the glossy matte paper. Hastily shifting it from one bin of chemical to another, I let my muteness fill your own thoughts. Eventually I sparked a conversation over Kubrick and you, animated by this acutely magnificent allusion, responded with an intrigue I pray haunted you like it did me. We developed over this time, like my rudimentary photographs. With years I came to treasure our brushing sleeves. I beside you, small and yearning to be attached. We worked silently beside each other, and I took pleasure in our shared time. Once, you held me in your camera, and I made certain that my painful love could be seen.

Through these years I found manifold devastations to grant myself. Between whiskey binges and railroad excursions. Underneath the weight of some skinny boy, I felt some deep vengeance against my unfulfilled love for you. Now I am old, I dream of our building, its architecture fused with the trappings of its paths. I am so goddamned afraid of when I get truly old, when I repeat old stories and shriveled jokes as a password and signal to my fellow geriatrics in the dim yellowness of a retirement home.

On my way home one day in winter, I kicked and crushed a clump of ice on the sidewalk. You were a man who people in your life reprimanded. They said you talked louder than you realized. You were deaf to your own booming voice. Yet unbeknownst to them, the volume of your words were merely the tidal force of passion you were oppressed by. Only you knew that you knew this. But I did too.

In the city I passed the Chinese joint: Happy Garden. Then the car wash: Bubble Tunnel. I saw Meteora's autograph on the bridge. The safe haven a block from the doll museum. I glared through the bus window with the stringy length of my headphones stirring in my hands, pounding music into my head that I believed, so tenderly, could awaken the passion in me.

You were my muse. You still are. I can tell no one. They will laugh at me. They think of you as an adolescent dream of my past. I feel like a Gothic novel; a tale of seduction that culminates in the ruin of its two united characters. I am bent on an inclination of suicide. I revel in the blade on my skin you never kissed. Because I hate you. You are the only person on this earth that still surprises me, inspires me, in the cold erudite mortuary of an increasingly indebted education. Those professors taught me these words to articulate my war. I denounce the spirit; it will outlive and forget me.

My lover and my slave! Come here at once so I can adore you and invoke the Gods of Turmoil and its Angel Liars. My breath chilled with wine, it is all for you, my Venerable Paramour. Today I was slithering into your photos online and realized you don't have chest hair. This observation destroyed me and all the imaginary encounters with you I had invested myself into. I saw your pale stomach and felt my tongue swell behind my teeth. Your eyes were red, probably fucked up, and I relished in your freedom. I was proud of your joy. Felt myself and my past briefly, hobbling down streets in a pack of hooting drunks. Some invisible sound telling me that this was the greatest day of my life.

www.ingramcontent.com/pod-product-compliance
Lightning Source LLC
Chambersburg PA
CBHW021136110726
47900CB00002B/380